IF IT ISN'T LOVE

IF IT ISN'T LOVE

TANYA TAYLOR

Three Little Birds Publishing
Houston, TX

IF IT ISN'T LOVE
This book is a work of fiction. Names, characters, places, and
incidents are the product of the author's imagination or are
used fictitiously. Any resemblance to actual events, locales,
or persons, living or dead, is strictly coincidental.

ISBN: 978-0-578-53774-0

Published by Three Little Birds Publishing
Houston, TX

Printed in the United States of America
First Edition October 2019
Cover Design by: Make Your Mark Publishing Solutions
Interior Layout by: Make Your Mark Publishing Solutions
Editing: Make Your Mark Publishing Solutions

ACKNOWLEDGEMENTS

I would like to acknowledge my mother, Martha, who is a constant source of love and support. My sister, Sheena, who has always been my biggest fan. My Aunt, Kathleen, who continues to push my literary talent and always tells me what's real rather than what's popular. My "brother" James for loving me and believing in me. You were the first person to purchase a copy of *If It Isn't Love*. To all those who have seen me through this journey, I thank each and every one of you. Monique D. Mensah with Make Your Mark Publishing Solutions, thank you for pushing me and encouraging me to share my voice and my story with the world.

I thank God for seeing me through one of the darkest and most painful times of my life. Although I couldn't see it at the time, those tough times set the play in motion for me to reach this point in my life, shaping me into a mother, teacher, author, and advocate for all those who have suffered at the hands of someone else.

CHAPTER ONE

The More Things Change ...

Constance was certain that, although Yvette's baby shower was today, somehow, someway, the topic of discussion would rear its intrusive head toward her love life. She had thought about faking an illness to avoid attending the event but realized that would be socially unacceptable since Yvette was her best friend and Constance was the hostess. All she could do was bite the bullet and prepare for the inevitable.

She stood in the middle of her closet for a while, wondering what to wear for the day's event. She finally decided on a brown and white dip-dyed shirtdress and a pair of gold open-toed sandals. She gave a smile of approval as she examined herself in the three-way mirror. Constance never thought herself conceited; however, she always felt she had a nice body and pretty face. Her natural auburn hair and stunning emerald eyes added to her beauty. She was lean with a runner's physique and stood a fluid 5'8". Turning to view her profile, she gave her stomach a slight pat, mentally noting to add more crunches to her workout regimen. With one last look, she was out the door and on her way to pick up the dessert for the shower.

Constance arrived at the bakery with time to spare. She eyed the decadent and delicious pastries behind the glass as she waited for her order. There were éclairs, lady-fingers, and petit fours, but this bakery was famous for its cupcakes. For the baby shower, Constance handpicked a beautiful tres leche cupcake with buttercream icing. On top of each cupcake was a cute figurine of an African American baby with its head peeking from beneath a receiving blanket made of pink fondant. As the cashier presented the cupcakes, Constance examined their quality and began to get lost in her thoughts.

Lately, it seemed her biological clock was ticking, and she didn't know how much longer she could continue to ignore it. Thirty-five was quickly approaching, and her window of opportunity had a limited lifespan.

She was making her way to the counter to pay when she locked eyes with a familiar face.

Oh, great! she thought.

"Hey, baby. Surprised to see you here." Antonio flashed the million-dollar smile he knew she couldn't resist, his local drawl resonating like music in her ears.

The two had met during their freshman year of college. He had promised her the world and never paid up. Even after he became engaged and married to someone else, Constance remained loyal to him because, deep down, she believed they were soulmates who had just met at the wrong time. They carried on an illicit love affair for years until she got serious about Marvin, deciding it was time for her to have a man of her own instead of borrowing someone else's.

As he stepped closer, the intoxicating scent of his cologne weakened her knees. Constance found herself gazing into his chestnut eyes and examining the features on his honey colored skin. She marveled at his broad shoulders and toned physique, searching for something that would make him less desirable while secretly admiring him at the same time. Constance knew exactly where her current state of mind could lead, and it was not a place she cared to revisit. The best way to handle Antonio was to be direct and leave. She had to play a calm hand, or he would see right through her façade.

"Listen," Constance said through tight lips, "I don't have time for small talk. I have a very important event to attend."

"That's cool, baby," Antonio said, placing his hand on Constance's arm. "I saw you and just wanted to say hi to my favorite girl. I'm glad I bumped into you, though. I haven't been able to talk to you since you went and changed your number. And you've stopped responding to my emails. I'm not gonna lie, my feelings were hurt. You know I never forgot about you … or the good times we had." He leaned in closer, placing his hand firmly around her waist, and she quickly removed it.

"Why waste your time dwelling on the past? I sure don't," she snapped.

"Come on, boo-boo, don't be so harsh. How are things going between you and that lawyer dude? Is he taking good care of you? 'Cause if he isn't, you know I can take *real* good care of you." Antonio licked his lips with delight. "You know nobody can work that fine body of yours the way I did. We fit together like a lock and key."

Antonio was right, and they both knew it. He caressed her arm, and Constance instantly grew moist. She allowed a smile to escape her lips, secretly entertaining the idea of him devouring her body one more time. However, before their conversation could go any further, Antonio's wife, Monique, manifested her way near them. A situation like this could result in an ugly scene, but Constance knew the drill, and Antonio was as smooth as silk. He slid his hand down Constance's arm and began to shake her hand.

"Well, it was sure good to see you again," he said with a twinkle in his eye.

"Likewise," Constance replied, tongue in cheek. She smiled at Monique and gave a very pleasant but fake "Hello."

"Constance?" Monique asked with more excitement than Constance felt necessary. "I haven't seen you since graduation! How have you been?"

"I've been well," Constance replied through a forced smile. She had no desire to hold a conversation with Antonio's wife.

"It was good to see you, Antonio. Y'all take care."

Just as Constance was about to exit with her purchase, she noticed Monique's protruding baby bump. "My, my! I didn't know the two of you were expecting." She threw Antonio a glare.

"Yes, girl. Two more months to go," Monique replied, beaming.

"A boy or girl?"

"A boy. Antonio Jr. He's gonna grow up and be just like his daddy."

Constance thought, *Lord, I hope not.*

"As a matter of fact," Monique continued, "we're having Antonio's birthday party at the house next weekend. You should come since the two of you are such good friends."

Is she serious? "Oh I don't—"

Antonio cut Constance off before she could finish her sentence. "Yeah, baby, that's a great idea! It'll give us a chance to catch up and talk about some old times." He gave Constance a wink.

Antonio seemed quite pleased with himself, and he kissed Monique on the cheek. Monique smiled with adoration for her husband.

"And we're not taking no for an answer," he added with a sly grin.

"But my shop—" Constance started.

"Please, you own the damn thing, don't you? What's so good about being your own boss if you can't take a day off?" Antonio smiled.

He always had a way of getting what he wanted, and

Constance knew that he was going to get her to come to that party, even if it meant driving her there himself. She was so angry she could spit fire.

"It seems I can't say no," was all she could muster.

"Good," replied Monique. "I'll have Antonio call you with all the details."

Constance pulled her business card holder from her bag. As she handed the card to Monique, Antonio conveniently intercepted and read it aloud.

"Essentials. Styles that take you from the office straight to happy hour. Constance McGuire, Owner."

"I'll have to stop by sometime after I have the baby," Monique added, rubbing her stomach.

Constance couldn't take much more of their idle chit-chat. Besides, she had all the information she needed. "I'm sorry, but I'm actually on my way to a baby shower I'm hosting."

"Okay, girl. It was good to see you," Monique said.

"You, too," Constance lied, sizing up the happy couple as they left. Monique was a pretty woman, petite in stature, and she glowed luminously from her pregnancy. Constance didn't understand why Antonio was so fixated on their past relationship, but she didn't let the thought linger. She paid for her cupcakes and scurried out of the bakery.

Constance arrived at Yvette's house precisely at noon and used her emergency key to let herself in. She knew she would find Yvette agonizing over every detail. Entering the living room, she noticed Yvette was making sure all the balloons held the same amount of helium. That was Yvette's way. She could be a little neurotic at times, but she was loyal and honest, which was hard to come by in a friend.

"Hey, crazy lady," Constance called out.

Her very round friend turned to her with a smile. Her statuesque 5'11" copper frame remained intact, even in pregnancy. She'd added only a few digits to her usual 190 pounds and had begun to wear her natural hair, convinced the chemicals from the relaxers would seep into her bloodstream and harm the baby. Her hair was growing like a weed. Most days, she wore it in a full Afro, but today, she sported Fulani braids, adorned with jewels. Yvette and Constance met in college, where Yvette also met her husband, Steve. By the end of their senior year, the two were married and living in wedded bliss. Constance never understood why Yvette cut herself off from the fabulous single world so early on, but lately, she began to envy her best friend's life: the house, the husband, the baby—Yvette seemed to have it all.

"My, my," Yvette sang. "Don't we look expensive," she said, referring to Constance's ensemble.

"You like?" Constance gave a twirl. "I got it in New York while on vacation with Marvin."

Yvette's smile quickly went cold.

Constance made a point not to acknowledge her friend's reaction and changed the subject. "So, what do you need me to do? I have two different itineraries printed out and ready to go, one for setup and one for the shower. So if you like, we can just follow these."

Yvette smiled and shook her head. "I don't know why you didn't go into event planning. You would've been great."

"Please, all those bridezillas, ladies who lunch, and birthday brats would've gotten on my nerves. But wait ... I have those same customers now, so maybe what you're saying isn't such a bad idea."

The two laughed and carried on with their itinerary.

Constance was hosting the shower, but Yvette insisted she help after all Constance had done for her last year. This was Yvette's second pregnancy; her first baby was stillborn. There was a funeral; however, Steve didn't attend. He said he couldn't stand to see his baby put into the ground. Yvette spiraled into a crippling depression shortly after. She wouldn't eat or sleep, and she spent most of the days crying. Steve was at a loss for how to handle the situation, so he immersed himself into his work. The first month was the most difficult. Constance took a leave from work and moved in with her friend to care for her. She brushed Yvette's teeth, fed her, bathed and dressed her, and combed her hair. Many nights, Constance held her friend as she sobbed until she fell asleep.

Their friend Tameka had come by a few times but always left abruptly. When Constance confronted her about her lack of sympathy and interest for their grieving friend, she replied, "Yvette has a husband. I figure she'd rather have him there. I don't want to invade their personal space." Tameka never minced her words.

The two friends were setting the last of the table arrangements when Constance turned to Yvette and blurted, "I ran into Antonio today."

"Really," was all Yvette uttered. She hated the fact that Constance and Antonio were even remotely involved.

"Monique is having a baby."

"What!" Yvette's mouth almost hit the floor. "And how does that make you feel?"

"I don't know ... relieved, confused, sad, jealous ..."

"What does she have for you to be jealous of? Antonio is a liar and a cheater. Why would you want that?"

Constance released a huge sigh. "I don't know. I mean she's having a baby with a man I was romantically involved with and still have some feelings for. It was hard enough for me when they got married, but now ..."

"I thought you two weren't messing around anymore." Yvette threw Constance a look that said, "You know better," the kind of look only a mother could give. "You knew what it was when you chose that lifestyle, chasing a sexual fantasy, living for the moment and not caring who you may hurt in the process. I'm sorry, Connie, but you have no right to be jealous. That man was never yours to begin with. You chose to be with Marvin, flaws and all. You can't jump out of the frying pan and into the fire. Better yet, Connie, take some time to yourself. You've been in relationships for as long as I've known you. Do you ever stop to think about what it is you want and not who your parents want you to be? You can't keep trying to live up to their expectations."

The doorbell interrupted their conversation, and Constance couldn't have been more relieved. She was not in the mood for one of Yvette's lectures. She got enough of that from her parents.

The two women went to greet the first guest.

There stood Tameka more than an hour late. "Well, ladies, I've finally arrived."

"Yeah, and not a moment too soon," Constance quipped. "We finished setting up fifteen minutes ago."

"I'm sorry. I just thought since you were the one planning this soirée, you'd be able to handle everything. I didn't see the need for me to come over here and get in the way."

Constance rolled her eyes. Typical Tameka, always thinking of herself. One would think that after an over twenty-year friendship, she wouldn't be so selfish, but her parental situation always gave her a sense of entitlement.

When Tameka was a baby, a wealthy family adopted her. They were one of few black families to reside in the upscale, exquisitely posh River Oaks District. Being a token and an only child made Tameka think the world revolved around her. All Tameka knew about her birth parents was that her black mother was a prostitute and her Cuban father was her pimp. She always said she didn't know or care about her biological parents, but Constance knew better than to believe that.

The fact that she was stunningly beautiful didn't help

her personality much. Tameka's skin was the color of coffee, black, no sugar or cream. She had the most beautiful gray eyes, glistening white teeth, and a luxurious coif of dark curls that fell past her shoulders. Constance envied how Tameka was always so sure of herself. She walked to the beat of her own drum and lived her life the way she wanted. Constance wished she were bold enough to do that, but she was too afraid of being an embarrassment to her family. Her mother was big on appearances. No matter how bad things were behind the scenes, Mrs. McGuire would tell her to put on a happy face and shine because people were watching them and looked to their family for guidance.

"So, what have I missed?" Tameka asked.

Constance motioned to Yvette to keep quiet without a word. She loved Tameka dearly, but she had a way of throwing salt on a wound, and Constance was just not in the mood today.

"Nothing much," Yvette said. The doorbell rang again. "Let's get this show on the road!"

After two hours and several hundred "Oh, how cutes," the baby shower was finally over. Yvette told her friends not to worry about cleaning up since the housekeeper would be in first thing in the morning. That was all Tameka needed to hear before she rushed to leave.

Constance gathered her things as Yvette walked Tameka to the door. Tameka disarmed the alarm on her luxury SUV, jumped in, and sped off. Constance was on her way out when Yvette stopped her at the threshold. She placed one hand on Constance's shoulder and looked her squarely in the eyes.

"Listen, Connie, I know you're a grown woman who's capable of making her own decisions. This life you have is yours and yours alone, and every decision you make impacts it."

Constance knew her friend was serious because she saw it in her eyes. However, she also knew Yvette couldn't understand the physical and emotional connection she shared with Antonio. It was only by circumstance the two of them weren't together.

She smiled at her friend's words. "I know."

Constance got into her car and drove off. She looked in the rearview mirror and noticed Yvette was waiting for her to turn the corner. Constance couldn't wait to get home because she knew that was the only place she could go and cry in peace.

CHAPTER TWO

... The More They Stay the Same

Second Sundays were always Constance's favorite. Those were the days she sang in the choir at her father's church. She'd been singing there since she was four years old and watched the church grow from its first fifty members to the one thousand members it celebrated today. She loved the diversity of the people who attended the services. True Vine's congregation was comprised of members ranging from bus drivers, to schoolteachers, to some of the top professionals in the city. Yvette, Steve, and Tameka were all members, too. For Constance, True Vine was home.

The soprano soloist had finished a powerful performance, and the Spirit was so high that the ushers and greeters had to fan some of the attendants. After the Spirit passed, the secretary delivered the announcement for visitors. She instructed all visitors to stand, and Constance waited for the usual hesitations, but much to her surprise, a young man immediately stood, and she took notice.

The first thing Constance observed was how fine the visitor was. He had the face of Adonis and beautiful skin the color of a pitch-black night. He stood well over six feet and had perfectly manicured chest-length locs styled into one thick French braid. His shoulders were straight and broad, his physique, muscular and girthy. Next, she examined his beautifully tailored suit draping his body like a second skin, not too tight but sized to perfection.

Impressive, she thought.

The nameless man turned many heads in the congregation. Constance noticed several of the female members break their necks to get a glimpse. He had to be the most gorgeous man she had ever seen.

"I've got to meet him," Constance uttered in awe.

"What?" Yvette leaned in closer to hear what her friend was saying.

"I've got to meet that man," she repeated.

Yvette used a paper fan to hide her mouth. "What man?" she asked from behind her disguise.

"That man with the beautiful dark locs. He is gorgeous!"

Yvette surveyed the crowd. "Oh, him ... He's okay."

Constance turned to Yvette. "Did you become blind after you got married? I don't know what you see, but I see one hell of a hunk."

Yvette nudged Constance for swearing. "And what about Marvin?" she asked.

The musical introduction began to play, and Constance shot up from her seat. "Sorry, I can't talk now. I've got a solo to sing," she replied with a smirk.

The congregation applauded as she made her way to the microphone. She closed her eyes, said a silent prayer, took a deep breath, and belted a moving solo. By the end of the song, the congregation had caught the Spirit again. Even Constance was in tears.

After service, Constance returned her choir robe and made her way back to the sanctuary with intentions to introduce herself to the handsome visitor. But to her surprise, she ran into Marvin. He looked quite dapper in his designer suit and shoes, although that was how he looked every day. Constance could not recall a time she had ever seen him in jeans. He always wore either a suit, slacks, or chinos, and he never went without a collared shirt. She found his attire his most attractive quality.

When they'd met in college, Marvin didn't carry himself like many of the other rapper wannabes she had been meeting. He dressed well, spoke well, was highly ambitious, and handsome to boot. To her, Marvin wasn't stop-traffic fine, but he wasn't unattractive. He was what southerners called "high yellow" and proud of it. He was average height, slim yet toned, and possessed delicate features: small eyes, a button nose, and slight pink lips. He sported a mane of soft, dark curly hair. He was the quintessential all-American BAP (Black American prince), the perfect young man to bring home and meet your parents.

"Marvin, what are you doing here?" she asked, looking

over his shoulder at the stranger as women bombarded him.

"I came home early to surprise you. So, are you surprised?"

"Surprised is an understatement."

Marvin took Constance by the hand. "I came in during your solo. You probably didn't see me because I didn't sit in our usual spot."

Constance looked over at the stranger, who was now on his way out the door.

Marvin's voice interrupted her gawking. "Well, baby, let's go."

"Where are we going?" she asked.

Marvin began to smile. "I told Mother we would come over for Sunday dinner."

"Well, I told Yvette I would go with her today to look at furniture for the nursery."

Marvin's eyes grew wide. "Well, what do you propose I tell Mother?"

You can tell her I hate her cooking, Constance thought but didn't dare say. "Well, sweetie," Constance put on a smile, "how about I meet you after I'm done?"

"But I told her you would be there." Marvin's tone had changed. His eyes narrowed, his brow furrowed. "What am I supposed to tell her when I show up without you?"

Constance knew where this was going, and she didn't want to cause a scene, especially at church.

"Marvin, let's talk outside."

"Why? Are you going to give me a different response once we're outdoors?"

She was about to speak, but Marvin cut her off.

"No, you're not. So why in the hell are we going outside? Why don't you just give me a call when you're done running the streets with your friend."

Constance was hurt. How dare he turn this into something it wasn't? She quickly decided not to feed into his tantrum. She gave Marvin a kiss on the cheek and told him she would call as soon as she got in.

He stormed out of the church.

"What was that all about?" Yvette asked.

"Same old, same old," Constance said, trying to hide the tears welling up in her eyes.

Yvette let out a heavy sigh and shook her head. "Connie, how long are you going to accept his little tantrums?"

Irritated, Constance quickly changed the subject. "Not now, okay. Where's Tameka?"

"Oh, she's waiting for us by the doors."

As the two women made their way to the doors, they noticed Tameka conversing with one of the newly appointed ushers. Constance and Yvette stood back and looked on. They noticed the young man had given Tameka his card and gave her a kiss on the cheek as he made his way back to the sanctuary. The two rushed over to Tameka as soon as he was out of sight.

"What was that all about?" Yvette asked.

"Now, you know it's a sin to gossip," Tameka teased.

"Oh, yeah," Constance jeered. "I'm pretty sure it's also

a sin to seduce a man in church, but you don't seem to have any trouble doing that."

"Why do you always have to do me like that, Connie? How do you know he wasn't trying to seduce *me*?"

"Because I know you," Constance joked.

Tameka's lip twitched. "And what the fuck is that supposed to mean?"

"Tameka, you will *not* use that foul language in God's house!" Yvette chided.

"Connie, you're always trying to put yourself above me!" Tameka whined.

"Girl, it was a joke. Calm down. We've been friends far too long for you not to know when I'm joking. Now, can we please get going before the stores close? And I want to hear more about this issue."

The women made their way out of the church. Once in the car, Tameka began to dish. "Girl, you should've heard him talking about how beautiful my skin is and how, unlike most brothas, he appreciates a dark-skinned sister."

"He actually said that?" asked Yvette.

"That and then some," Tameka boasted. "He said he'd had his eye on me for a while and often wondered if my skin was as soft as it looked. We talked for a little while. He gave me his number and told me to be sure to use it sooner than later."

"Isn't he going to seminary school?" asked Yvette.

"Girl, that doesn't mean anything," Constance added. "After he becomes a pastor, he's going to need a catcher's mitt for all the coochie that will come his way. You know when a woman gets a preacher, she acts like she got a VIP pass to heaven, like being with a holy man makes her less soiled and worthier in God's eyes."

Tameka rolled her eyes. "Please, don't bring your family issues into this."

"Keep my family out your trifling-ass mouth!" Constance snapped. "I'm not Yvette. I won't pray for you. I'll beat you down and leave you bloody!"

"No, you won't," Yvette interjected. "Y'all are gonna argue and threaten each other like you always do and then make up and go shopping. So, are you going to call this man?" she asked Tameka, dismissing their spat.

"Hell yeah, I'm going to call him. He's fine! And did you see the size of his feet?"

The car exploded with laughter.

After an afternoon of shopping, the ladies stopped for a bite to eat, and Constance drove her friends home. She stuck to her word and called Marvin as soon as she made it to her condo. His voicemail picked up on the first ring.

"Hey, baby. It's me, calling like I said I would. I'm just letting you know I'm home. Call me. I love you."

Constance stepped out of her stilettos and poured herself a glass of Pinot Grigio before heading upstairs to draw a hot bath. She lit a few scented candles, played some sultry tunes on her speaker system, and inched her way into the scorching hot bath.

The foam from an effervescent ball tickled the crevices

between her thighs. Constance let out a soft moan as her mind drifted to Antonio. She thought about how good he looked the day before and how his words had rung true. Nobody could work her body like he could. Antonio was a beast in the bedroom. He was also an animal in the kitchen, the car, the elevator, or wherever he felt the mood.

Constance remembered the time she received a call from Antonio with strict instructions to meet him at his office wearing nothing but a coat and his favorite pair of black stilettos. It was the middle of a work day, but Constance didn't care. Anytime Antonio called, she went running. Within thirty minutes, she arrived at Antonio's office naked beneath a trench coat and *red* stilettos. She closed the door and let her coat hit the floor. Constance crawled onto his desk and spread eagle, exposing the soft pink folds between her legs. Antonio wasted no time and buried his face between Constance's Brazilian wax. He rose with lips glistening from her essence.

"The fuck I told you?" he said with deep, sensual aggression. "I told you to put on the *black* heels. What color are those shoes you have on?"

Constance smirked between heavy breaths, anticipating what was to come.

"Oh, so you think I'm playing? Bend over and spread your cheeks."

Constance did as instructed. She let out a heavy moan when she felt the moist heat from Antonio's mouth between her cheeks. He made sure to lather her bottom well.

"I see I'm going to have to teach you a lesson, and you better not cum until I tell you."

Antonio's steel penetrated her taut hole, sending a sensational pleasure through her entire body. He had a handful of Constance's hair in one hand as he cuffed her mouth with the other to muffle her screams.

Antonio pressed the weight of his body against Constance's back and whispered in her ear, "I'm about to cum, and I want you to cum with me."

He released himself into her hole, and Constance sprang like a faucet.

The memory made her nipples perk, and she began to caress her thighs, making her way to her erect clitoris. An explosion began to grow inside her. For a second, she felt guilty, as if she were cheating on Marvin, but then she remembered how Antonio liked to taste her juices, and her body began to tremble. Constance stroked her clit harder and faster than she had ever done before.

Her doorbell rang, but she ignored the sound. The memory of Antonio's lips dripping from her essence invaded her brain. The doorbell rang again, but Constance was on a mission. She caressed her clit faster. The bell rang rapidly, three more times. Whoever was at the door was determined to get in, yet, with each ring, Constance only stroked herself faster until she released an intense orgasm, sending a buzz of electricity flowing through her body.

The persistent doorbell quickly jolted her to her feet. She threw on her clothes and made her way downstairs to identify the intruder. She peered through the peephole and opened the door. There stood Marvin looking pissed as usual.

"What are you doing here?" she asked.

"You seem surprised. Am I interrupting something?" he asked.

"Just my bath. I called you. Why didn't you answer my call?"

"I'm here, aren't I?"

"Yes, you are, and unannounced, at that."

"Oh, so you can hang with your friends all day, but you can't make time for your man?"

Constance rolled her eyes. "Marvin, that's not what I'm saying ..."

"Well, that's what it sounds like," he growled. "I'm here, and I'm staying. I've been out of town for three days. The least you can do is screw me, since you don't want to spend any time with me."

"Is that what you're here for, sex?"

"Don't be ridiculous. I'm here because you're mine, and I want to spend time with you. Now, if I get some sex out of it, that would definitely make my drive over here worthwhile." Marvin approached Constance and placed his arms around her waist. "And with you standing here smelling and looking as good as you do, how could I possibly resist?"

Constance could feel Marvin's manhood growing in his pants.

"You see what you do to me?" he asked, placing a passionate kiss upon her lips. "All I want is to spend my evening with you and wake up to your beautiful face next to me. And if that's a crime, then consider me guilty."

After the episode in the bathtub, Constance was in no mood for sex with Marvin, especially since she knew it wouldn't measure up to her memories of Antonio. But if she wanted to prove to Marvin that she was worthy of being his wife, she'd have to learn to submit, a practice she'd learned from years of observing her parents' relationship.

Reluctantly, Constance led the way upstairs to her bedroom. While lying on her bed, she endured Marvin painfully tweaking her nipples. She was not turned on, not now, and not for the past six months. Sex with Marvin had grown mundane and routine. He would painfully pull on her nipples then kiss her neck. After that, he would turn over and wait for Constance to mount him. The whole thing would last about ten or fifteen minutes. Marvin was a lousy, lazy lay. Nevertheless, Constance's mother told her there were far more important things in a marriage than sex. She would just have to learn to make do with the sex Marvin offered. She waited for him to climax and pretended she'd done the same. He immediately fell asleep, snoring like a bear.

As Constance lay there listening to him snore, watching the drool escape the corner of his mouth, she thought, *Will it always be like this?*

CHAPTER THREE

Close Encounters

Constance's morning couldn't officially begin without a cup of coffee, and since there wasn't any in her pantry, she decided to grab a cup on her way to work. The parking lot at the local coffee spot was full, as usual. She circled the lot twice with no luck. The only spot she could find was too narrow. She cursed herself for not getting a two-seater.

Just as she was about to make yet another trip around the lot, a young, attractive blonde tapped on her car window.

"You need a spot?" she asked.

Constance nodded.

"Follow me."

She followed the woman to her vehicle and waited for her as she backed her car out of the parking space.

Constance had barely put the car into park before she jumped out to thank the stranger for being so kind.

"No problem," she replied, seemingly frazzled. "Mondays are a typical rat race."

Constance reached into her satchel, pulled out her business card, and scribbled on the back. She gave the card to the young woman. "Twenty percent off any purchase when you stop by my place."

The young woman accepted the card, with noticeably shaky hands. "Essentials. Hey, I've been meaning to stop in there. I always pass it on my way to the gym."

Constance told her to stop by soon, and the woman promised she would.

Upon entering the coffee shop, the aroma danced into Constance's nostrils and clung to the air. She ordered a grande latte and a bite to eat. She sat at a small corner table and began to review her email when a male voice interrupted.

"Excuse me, but don't you attend True Vine?"

She looked up from her tablet to acknowledge the voice in front of her. To her surprise, it was the visitor from church.

"Yes, I do," Constance replied, practically exposing all thirty-two teeth.

"I thought you looked familiar. I just wanted to tell you that your solo was righteous. I wanted to speak with you after service, but there was a mad mob of members approaching me."

"Yes, well, True Vine members are quite friendly. You have an interesting accent. I take it you're not from here."

The handsome gentleman smiled, revealing two dimples. "You're right. I'm from Trinidad, but I've lived most of my life in D.C. I'm Ahyende, by the way. Ahyende Ali."

"Pleasure to meet you, Ahyende. I'm Constance McGuire."

The two shook hands, and the hair on the back of Constance's neck stood up. His touch made her nervous yet excited. The two held hands longer than necessary and, finally, after what seemed like an eternity, they let go.

"Please, have a seat," Constance offered, her voice laced with saccharine.

"Thank you, but I don't want to intrude. I just saw you and had to come over to let you know how much your voice moved me."

She blushed. "Why, thank you, but it's no intrusion. I'm here alone."

As he sat, Constance caught a whiff of Ahyende's cologne. It was unusual but tantalizing. He smelled of amber and woodsy notes with a hint of soap. She looked down and noticed that his nails were short and clean.

Constance broke their silence. "So, what made you stop by True Vine?"

"Well, I just recently relocated here. My mother calls me every Sunday and asks if I've found a church, and she's always disappointed when I tell her no, which is highly unacceptable for the son of a preacher. So I asked some of my clients where they attend, and I was led to True Vine."

Constance began to laugh and Ahyende laughed, too.

"I'm sorry, did I miss something," he asked.

"It's just that you mentioned your father is a preacher. I'm a P.K., too. True Vine is my father's church."

"P.K.?" he asked with a raised brow.

"Preacher's kid."

"Oh! Well, one day, we'll have to swap stories of our rebellion."

"Oh, I don't have any," Constance confessed. "I'm a daddy's girl. I never did anything that could get back to my father and disappoint him. My mama would always tell me that any shame I brought upon myself, I also brought upon my daddy and the church. I was expected to carry myself as a McGuire first, a lady second, and a child of God always."

"Well, I'm sure my parents would have traded me in for you in a heartbeat. Growing up, I gave my mother and father all kinds of hell. My father has been deceased five years now, but when I was a teen, I had a hard time following the rules of the church. In my 'hood, it wasn't cool to be a boy who was saved and holy. I had to do what the other homies did, or else they would think I was a punk."

The two laughed. At that moment, Constance's phone rang. She looked to see who it was. It was Marvin, and he couldn't have had worse timing. He was gone long before she had awakened, and she hadn't bothered to call him to see why he left so early.

"It's my mother," she lied. "I'll call her back when I make it in to work. You mentioned clients. What line of business are you in?" she asked, quickly guiding the conversation back toward the previous topic.

"Well, you can say I'm in the world's oldest profession."

Concern stretched across Constance's face, and Ahyende laughed.

"I'm a carpenter. I design and sell furniture. Nothing extravagant. I have an online store with a nice clientele; however, I'm working on getting my own space. For now, I work out of a studio I'm renting."

Constance let out a chuckle. "You know, for a minute, I thought you were about to tell me you were some sort of gigolo."

"I just met you, but believe me when I say you would not have to pay me for my time. I'd give every second of it to you for free."

Constance was flattered and quickly becoming smitten with the gentleman she had just met.

"So, what is it *you* do?" Ahyende asked.

"I own a boutique called Essentials. You should check it out some time." She gave Ahyende her business card.

He read the card and placed it inside his wallet.

Constance checked the time on her watch. "I'm sorry, but I really have to get going. It has been very nice chatting with you."

"I completely understand. I have some orders I need to finish, but it has been a real pleasure. Maybe we can do this again some time."

"Maybe," Constance replied.

She grabbed her bag and made her way to the door.

As she left, she glanced over her shoulder and noticed Ahyende was watching as she exited. She turned back around and made sure to put a little extra switch in her hips as she walked out the door.

Constance made it to work just before opening. Alicia, her assistant manager, was busy going about the day's business, reviewing numbers and payroll, while Keith, the visual merchandiser, worked on the new window displays. Alicia had been with Constance since she opened her business. The two hit it off immediately and became fast friends. Keith came onboard shortly after Alicia, and the rest was retail history.

Constance walked in sporting a huge grin. "Good morning," she said in a sing-song voice.

Alicia looked up from the registers and noticed Constance grinning like a Cheshire cat. "Girl, you must have gotten you some before work because you are bursting with energy and cheerfulness today."

"Am I? I didn't notice." Constance merely shrugged off the observation.

"So, Miss Priss, what's up with the extra pep in your step?" Alicia inquired as Constance walked toward the office.

"I have no idea what you mean," she replied coolly.

"Sure, you don't," Alicia remarked. "Marvin must have done something right ... *this* time, anyway."

Constance threw Alicia a glare and decided to keep

her little encounter with Ahyende to herself. After all, there was nothing to tell.

Soon, the doors to the store were open, and business began. By noon, the store was booming with the lunch crowd. Constance thought all day about her encounter with Ahyende, the way he smelled, the sparkle in his eyes, the way she felt when they touched. She had to get it together. Why was she thinking about Ahyende when she had a man? She went into her office to call Marvin.

"It's about time you called," he hissed.

"Well, hello to you, too."

"What took you so long to call me?"

Constance grew defensive. "I've been busy with work."

"I know you can't be that busy selling clothes. I want you to meet me for dinner. I already made the reservations for seven o'clock."

"I can't. I'm closing tonight."

"Have someone else stay. Look, I've been spending a lot of time working, and this is my way of making it up to you. So Constance, will you please grace me with your presence tonight for dinner?"

Marvin always said what Constance wanted to hear. She sighed and gave in. "I'll have to go home first. You can pick me up from there."

She didn't want to ask Alicia to stay and do a twelve-hour shift but, surprisingly, she agreed without giving her any sass.

That evening, they arrived at the restaurant at precisely seven o'clock. The two laughed and talked while they enjoyed their meal. Marvin ordered his usual filet mignon, and Constance ordered penne pasta with sun dried tomatoes and a salad. He suggested she order a meal with more "class," perhaps lobster or sole, but Constance didn't see the difference.

"Any common person can order pasta," he explained. "And there is nothing common about us."

Over dessert, Marvin stared lovingly into Constance's eyes. "Connie," he said, "I have a surprise for you."

Her eyes lit up. She loved surprises. Her daddy would always bring her a gift home from his church travels, and it was as if he had brought her a sack of gold every time he returned. Constance loved her mother, but she was a daddy's girl and, in her eyes, he could do no wrong.

"Can I have it right now?" She was as giddy as a kid in a toy store.

"Calm down. You'll get it all in due time."

Constance couldn't wait to leave.

Once inside the car, she set the radio to her favorite R&B station. The smooth sounds of Luther Vandross and Cheryl Lynn's "If This World Were Mine" floated through the speakers. Luther was one of those crooners who could make her panties drop. She turned up the volume and closed her eyes while she sang along to the words. An image of Ahyende inadvertently popped into her head, and she let out a warm, soft sigh.

"You thinking about me, baby?" Marvin asked with confidence.

Constance was roused from her daydream. "Huh?"

"I see you over there smiling and singing along to the song."

She looked over at Marvin, who was wearing a huge smile. "Of course," she replied with a crooked grin.

Marvin seemed pleased with her lie, but it didn't take long to revert to his old ways. "Why aren't you holding my hand?"

"I don't know. I was just enjoying the ride."

"So, you wouldn't enjoy the ride if you were holding my hand?"

What the hell is he thinking?

The evening had been going so well, and she didn't want to do anything to spoil it. So, to keep the peace, she reached out and held Marvin's hand. He looked pleased once again.

"You need to learn to appreciate your man," he lectured, sounding more like a father figure than a boyfriend.

They drove the rest of the way in silence.

By the time they made it to Marvin's townhouse, Constance had calmed her nerves. She had been so upset that she'd almost forgotten about her surprise.

She broke the silence. "Earlier, you mentioned something about a surprise?" she asked as sweetly as she could.

"It's right behind this door. But first, you have to tell me how much you love me."

"Marvin, please, you know how much I love you." She

pressed her body against his and placed her hand over the bulge in his pants as she lathered him with passionate kisses.

Marvin fumbled with the lock as he attempted to open the door. Constance began to take off his blazer and unbutton his shirt as they made their way into the house. She was startled once they reached the end of the hall. Someone had flipped on the lights, and at least fifteen people emerged from the darkness.

"Surprise!"

Constance was so startled that she screamed. She surveyed the room as she caught her breath. Right there in the middle of Marvin's living room stood Yvette, Tameka, Alicia, Marvin's mother, and Constance's parents amongst a slew of Marvin's close friends and colleagues.

"What are y'all doing here?" Constance asked. She was at a total loss. It wasn't her birthday nor was it anyone else's. She had no clue what was going on.

She took one more look around the room and examined the looks on the guests' faces, trying to gather some sense of what was happening. Everyone wore huge smiles, except her father, who sported a rather stoic expression.

Marvin took Constance by the hand and led her to the sofa. She looked at him and asked the question everyone else seemed to ignore.

"Marvin, what are all our friends and family doing here? This can't be the surprise."

He looked at her with a twinkle in his eye. "It is part of it," he replied. "You see, all these people are here because they know how much I love you and want to spend the rest of my life with you. They are here because they know that you are the only woman in the world for me." He positioned himself on one knee as he reached into his pocket and pulled out a small blue box. He opened the box, and inside sat a five-carat, emerald-cut, platinum engagement ring. "They are here to witness me ask you for your hand in marriage."

Constance couldn't believe what was happening. Here was Marvin on one knee in front of everyone close to them proposing marriage. She began to get overheated, and her ears started ringing. The next ten seconds seemed to last ten years.

Marvin cleared his throat. "Constance Marie McGuire, will you marry me?"

She examined the anticipating faces in the room, looked at the ring, and looked down at Marvin right before she hurled vomit all over his dress shirt. The entire room looked disgusted, everyone except Tameka, who chuckled.

"I'm sorry, everyone, but, suddenly, I don't feel so well. It must have been something I ate," Constance explained holding her stomach.

Constance's mother ran over to her. "Baby, are you okay? Do you need to lie down?" She leaned in closer to her daughter and whispered, "Are you pregnant?"

Constance gave her mother a sideways glance. "No, Mama, I'm not pregnant, but I would like for everyone to leave."

Marvin's guests left immediately while Constance's friends stood still.

She grew irritated. "I said I would like for *everyone* to leave!"

Pastor McGuire placed his arm around his wife. "Mildred, I believe it's best if we give Connie some space."

Marvin's mother gave Constance an ugly look. "Marvin, sweetie, do you want Mama to stay around and help clean up?"

"Sure, Mom. The soap—"

"I need everyone to get the hell out!" Constance was no longer playing nice. "Mrs. Wallace, *I* made the mess, and *I* will clean it up."

"Well, it's the least you could do," she said in her usual condescending tone.

Her remark did not sit well with Constance's mother. Sure, she was a preacher's wife, but she didn't stand for anyone disrespecting her child.

"And just what is that supposed to mean?" Mrs. McGuire snapped, standing with her hand on her hip.

"Oh, Mildred, please," replied Mrs. Wallace. "Let's not get ethnic. That daughter of yours should have better manners. I'm quite sure her brash behavior has highly embarrassed the good reverend."

That was all the fuel Mrs. McGuire needed. The night ended with Marvin taking his mother to the emergency room because Mildred had knocked out Mrs. Wallace's front tooth.

That night, as she lay in bed, Constance analyzed her reaction to Marvin's proposal. Why didn't she just say yes? After all, she *did* love him. Sure, she may not have been head over heels in love, but that was not as important as what he could bring to the marriage. How could she have the family she'd always dreamed of without having the man? Her head was swimming with questions. She would just have to deal with it in the morning. Right then, she had to get some sleep.

It was seven a.m., and Constance's phone was ringing off the hook. She looked at the caller ID: private number.

"Now what?" she said aloud to herself. "Hello?"

"Oh, good. You answered your phone. I didn't think you would with it being so early and all."

"Then why did you call," she spat. "And who is this?"

"Oh, baby, my feelings are hurt."

Now, she could identify the early ringer. "Antonio, why are you calling me this early, and how did you get my home number? It isn't printed on my business card."

"Girl, you know I work magic."

"Yeah, right," she replied. "You're probably screwing some girl who works for the phone company."

"Hey, it helps to have connections," Antonio responded with a laugh. "Anyway, I was calling to let you know the party is Saturday at seven. It's at my place. You remember how to get there?"

Constance was the one who had helped him pick out the house, and Monique had no idea. "Yeah, I remember, and I'll be there. Can I bring a guest?"

"Oh, you know me, baby, I don't cock block. Besides, I know your kitty prefers me. That suit-and-tie geek can't put it down the way I did."

"Please, that was years ago."

"What can I say? Your kitty made a huge impression on me."

She ended the call and grabbed her pillow, pressing it against her face as she let out a muffled scream. *My day has to get better.*

Constance arrived at work, looking stunning as usual, wearing a scarf-print maxi dress and a pair of jeweled sandals.

Alicia stood at the cash registers, brimming with excitement. "Girl, what happened to you last night? I've never witnessed anything like that."

Constance tried to give her an explanation, but instead let out a roar of laughter. "Well, that depends. Are you speaking of my regurgitation or my mama knocking Mrs. Wallace's tooth under the table?"

"Both! And Yvette and Tameka have been calling all morning."

"Yeah, I figured that much. Those two and my mother have been blowing up my cell. I've had too much going on this morning to call them back."

ILOR

"Well, have you at least talked to Marvin?"

"No, but I'm sure I will."

"Uh oh," Alicia warned. "I think I may have spoken too soon."

Marvin came storming through the door. "Constance, I need to speak with you, now." His tone was stern as always.

She led him into the office so they could talk privately.

Constance set off a verbal explosion before Marvin could say a word. "Marvin, baby, I'm so sorry about my mother. Both our parents were out of line. As for what I did, I guess it was just my nerves. I mean I knew this would happen one day, but I just didn't think it would happen last night. I love you, and I hope you don't doubt that. All I'm asking for is some time. I need to sort out my reaction to your proposal."

She finally let Marvin speak. "Constance, it's fine. I understand that it was all so sudden. Just keep this ring while you think. Try it on. See how you like it; maybe it will grow on you. I will calm Mother down. Next time, you'll just have to make sure your mother acts right. She *is* a preacher's wife, for Christ's sake. Anyway, darling, I'm glad we had this discussion, and I'm sure that, with time, you will see that I am the best thing for you. You just aren't clever enough to realize that yet."

Constance didn't know what to say. But she didn't want any more chaos between the two of them, so she made no remark. Instead, she just smiled and walked Marvin to the door.

38

"Connie, before I leave, I wanted to invite you to dinner tonight. I'm meeting some clients, and I hope you'll be wearing your ring." Marvin gave her a kiss on the cheek and left the store.

"My, my! Have we made up?" Alicia said.

Constance rolled her eyes and ignored her comment. "What happened while I was off the floor," she asked.

"Not much. Keith came in. Don't worry, I filled him in on last night's juicy details, and Tameka is on line one. Yvette, on line two."

Constance made her way to the phone to reassure both friends she was not pregnant and she and Marvin were fine. She wanted to invite Tameka to Antonio's party as her buffer but decided to wait until later.

The rest of the day carried on normally. Constance was busy reviewing the store's sales when the door chime sounded. Alicia greeted the customer and made her way over to Constance.

"Girl, I just met my future husband," Alicia gushed.

Constance continued with her paperwork, paying Alicia's remark little attention. It seemed that since Alicia turned twenty-five, every good-looking man she met who wasn't wearing a ring was her "future husband."

"Girl, he is tall and fine. I'm gonna go see if he needs any help."

"Please do," said Constance as she kept on with her paperwork. "After all, that is what I pay you to do."

"And not very much," Alicia snipped.

"Alicia, listen to me. You just met this man thirty

seconds ago. If he's in here, he's either married, involved, or gay, which means he's probably here to see Keith."

"Oh no, Miss McGuire, you are not going to talk me out of this one. Besides, all is fair in love and war. If he's taken, he'll tell me."

Before Alicia could make her way back, Keith was already making his move.

She quickly intercepted. "Keith, can you please unload the new boxes of shipment. I'll be more than happy to assist this gentleman with whatever he needs." Alicia smiled, batting her lashes.

"I'm sorry, but are you okay?" the man asked Alicia.

"Why wouldn't I be?"

"Well, I thought maybe you had something in your eyes."

Keith let out a cackle.

"Maybe I just like what I see," Alicia replied.

The customer stared at her blankly. "Okay. Is there anyone else who can help me? I'm actually looking for—"

"Alicia, I have to run an errand," Constance called out.

The customer looked over in her direction. "Constance!"

"Ahyende?" She tried to hide the excitement in her voice.

"Excuse me," Alicia interjected, "but how do you two know each other?"

They both just stood there, smiling.

"Hello?" Alicia urged.

Constance broke the silence. "Ahyende is a new member at my daddy's church."

"Well, I'm not a member yet, but I will be if you keep singing like you do."

Alicia could plainly see their attraction. The energy between the two of them was kinetic. Even Keith, who had been eavesdropping the entire time, noticed. Alicia knew immediately what had brought this brother into Essentials, and he found what he was looking for. She left the two of them alone but made sure to stay within earshot.

Constance couldn't contain her smile. Ahyende was looking good. He wore a white dress shirt with lilac pinstripes, a lavender paisley tie, gray slacks, and polished dress shoes. Just looking at him made her weak in the knees. Constance used the counter as balance for fear she might fall over.

"So, how are you?" he asked with a smile.

"I'm keeping busy and you?"

"I've been well. I was in the neighborhood and decided to stop by. I hope I'm not keeping you from business."

He moved in closer to her. Constance could feel her heart pounding inside her chest.

"I was actually on my way to the bank to make a deposit. It's not far from here. You can stick around until I get back."

Ahyende moved in even closer. He was so close she could smell the scent of peppermint on his breath.

"Look, I've never been one for pretense. The truth is I

came all this way to see if you would grace me with your presence and have lunch with me. I just had a meeting with a mortgage broker at the bank and noticed I was in the same neighborhood as your shop."

Before her brain could fully process what he'd said, she replied, "Sure, I'd like that. Let me grab my purse."

Constance went into the back office. "Connie, what are you doing?" she whispered to herself. "It's just a harmless lunch," she replied to her own question and headed out the door.

The two dined at a nearby quaint bistro. Over lunch, they chatted like old friends and discovered they had a lot in common. They shared the same taste in food, literature, and music, coining the late, great Luther Vandross as the greatest male singer of all time. Constance also learned that Ahyende had quit his career as a marketing director at an advertising firm in D.C. to pursue his passion for carpentry and woodwork. He had been living in the city for the past nine months and finally decided he needed to purchase a home instead of renting.

After an hour passed, their plates were clean, and the wine was gone. Ahyende motioned to the waiter for the check, and Constance went for her purse.

"What are you doing?" he asked.

"I was looking for my credit card so I can pay my half of the bill."

Ahyende's lips parted, displaying a dazzling white smile. He leaned over and placed his hand on hers. "Now, I know I'm not from the South, but what kind of gentleman would I be if I had you pay for your own meal? After all, I was the one who invited you."

Constance slowly removed her hand from his grasp and put her wallet back into her purse. "I didn't mean to offend you, it's just …"

"It's just that you didn't want this to feel like a date? Hey, it's cool."

"It's not like that at all. I truly believe in letting a man be a man, especially a brotha, but as a woman, an unmarried one at that, I have to set boundaries."

"See, that is why I'm so attracted to you. Not only do you have an angelic face and sexy body, but you also have a beautiful mind. There's so much more to you than meets the eye, and I want to get to know each and every part of you."

Constance knew this conversation had to come to a halt. She had already betrayed Marvin's trust by going out with another man.

"Ahyende, I have to be upfront with you. I have a boyfriend, and we've been in a committed relationship for the past seven years."

Ahyende looked at her with a smile that she was beginning to memorize. "Of course, you do. A sister such as yourself … A man would be a fool not to be with you. However, you are as intrigued with me as I am with you. Only thing is you don't know it yet, or maybe you do. Seven years, huh, and still no ring on that finger?"

Constance looked down at her bare hand with a pang of guilt in her chest.

The waiter came over, and Ahyende paid for the check. "So Constance, I guess this is our first and last lunch together. It was truly a pleasure meeting you."

"Likewise," she replied, standing to leave.

Ahyende stood as well. "Can I at least walk you to your car?"

"Thank you for offering, but there's no need. You have a wonderful day, Ahyende." She gave a warm smile and walked out the door.

Constance returned to work as if nothing happened. Even though Alicia kept pestering her for details, Constance would only reply that Ahyende was a friend. She continued with her day and left just in time to meet Marvin for dinner. While home, she showered and slipped on a slinky cocktail dress. She sprayed herself with her most expensive perfume and called Marvin to see if he was on his way.

"Hey, baby. I'm all dolled up and waiting for you to pick me up."

Marvin was silent on the other end.

"Hello? Marvin, are you there?"

"Yeah, honey, I'm here. Look, the time of the dinner changed. I tried to call you at work, but you'd left already."

Constance was puzzled. "And you couldn't have called my cell phone?"

"We'll have to finish this conversation later. I see the clients at the door."

"You're already at the restaurant?"

"Look, sweetheart, I have to go. Love you."

Constance was enraged. Beads of perspiration formed on her nose. She called Marvin again, but the phone went straight to voicemail. She didn't bother to leave a message. Instead, she poured herself a glass of Sauvignon Blanc and called Tameka.

"Hey, MeMe."

Tameka could hear the frustration in her friend's voice. "What did Marvin do now?" she asked.

"I don't want to talk about it. Just meet me at The Spot in an hour."

"That's cool," replied Tameka. "I was about to hook up with Jermaine. I'll just tell him the change of plans."

"Who the heck is Jermaine?" Constance asked, confused.

"Um, the usher from church."

Constance shook her head. "So you really did it, huh?"

"Yeah, and it was good." Tameka giggled. "I'll tell you all about it at The Spot."

CHAPTER FOUR

All Work and No Play

The heads of the male onlookers snapped as Constance pulled up to the valet. She stepped out of her ride looking like a million bucks. She had changed out of her cocktail dress into a black romper that cut down to her torso and a pair of freak 'em girl pumps. Her auburn coif hung freely past her shoulders, and in each ear shone a stunning chandelier earring.

The line to the club was as long as always, but Constance never waited in line. She sashayed her hips right up to the front door. She could see the sneers of the other women as she passed by. A few of them even uttered obscenities toward her under their breath. But Constance didn't care. She was used to it. She walked right up to the bouncer and gave him a kiss on the cheek as she slid him a fifty-dollar bill.

"Connie, baby, you know your money's no good with

me." Beau had a deep, savory voice like Ving Rhames with the bald head and muscles to match.

"What's wrong with me wanting to show some appreciation to my favorite bouncer?" she asked with a smile.

"Girl, you know you know me better than that. You used to be my girlfriend back in junior high."

"Yeah, I remember that. I also remember you had a lot more hair back then."

They both let out a laugh.

"Yeah," he replied, "and you damn sure didn't have all that ... well, you know." Beau's eyes moved up and down Constance's body. "But seriously, we're friends; I can't take this from you."

Constance placed her hand on Beau's shoulder. "I know all these tired folks aren't tipping you like they should. Just look at it like one friend helping another. If it makes you feel any better, you can take this tip from me now, and I'll never tip you again."

"Now, I didn't say all that."

"That's what I thought." She snickered and began heading toward the entrance.

"Hey, Connie," Beau called out to her, "you know you'll always be my girl." He leaned in and gave Constance a kiss on the cheek as he slid the fifty back to her. "Don't hurt nobody."

"I won't do too much damage," she replied.

Rhythmic sounds of R&B dance music filled the air as Constance walked into the club. People crowded the dance floor, moving in synchronicity to the lyrics, never missing a beat. Tameka was waiting at their usual spot by the stage, hugged up with her newfound love interest. Constance greeted her friend with a hug.

Tameka turned to Jermaine. "Baby, I want you to meet my best friend, Constance."

Jermaine smiled at Constance, exposing his open-faced gold tooth. Deacon No Good may have been a heathen, but the brotha could dress. His skin was milky, almost white. He had red hair, and freckles speckled his cheeks and nose. He wasn't drop-dead gorgeous but decent.

"I finally get a chance to meet boss man's beautiful baby girl." He reached out and gave Constance a hug. "Your daddy talks so much about you. I feel like we're family."

"Well, it's nice to meet you, too, Jerome," Constance lied.

"Oh, baby, the name is Jermaine, but I won't hold it against you, not unless you want me to." He laughed with a snort and reassured Tameka he was only joking.

Tameka turned to Jermaine. "Baby, how about you get us a drink?"

Jermaine seemed offended. "I thought that was what the waitress was for."

"Baby, please. I need to talk to my girl," Tameka coaxed.

"Oh, I get it. Y'all can't talk about me if I'm sitting here."

"Exactly," Tameka said. "Connie, what are you having?"

"I'll take a cranberry and vodka."

"All right," Jermaine replied and walked off.

"Jermaine!" Tameka called.

"Oh, yeah, baby, I didn't forget about you. What you drinking?"

Constance couldn't believe this guy.

As soon as he was out of earshot, Tameka turned to Constance to get her approval. "So, what do you think?" she asked with an eager grin.

Constance knew this was neither the time nor place to tell Tameka the truth. "He seems okay," she said with a feigned smile.

Tameka seemed pleased with Constance's response. "I knew you would like him. And don't he look sharp?"

"Yes, he *is* sharp."

Jermaine made his way back to the table. "My ears are burning," he said. He was beginning to work Constance's nerves.

"Yeah, baby, we were talking about how good you look in your new suit," Tameka said.

"Oh, you like this suit, Connie? It was specially bought for me by my baby."

Constance almost choked on her drink. "What?"

Tameka had a silly grin on her face. "Yeah, girl. I'm fly, so my man has to be fly, too."

Constance shook her head. No matter how much love Tameka's adoptive parents lavished on her, it never made up for the lost love of her biological parents, and it showed at times like this.

"MeMe, I need to check my makeup. Come with me."

Tameka got up and followed her friend. Her mouth ran like a faucet, talking about her new "boyfriend."

Constance had to cut her off. "Look, MeMe, how is this man treating you?"

"Oh, we're fine. Last night, we went and ate at Steak 48."

"Steak 48! Can he pay for a meal there?"

Tameka rolled her eyes. "He didn't; I did. And before you start lecturing me, keep in mind that I am a grown-ass woman, and I can spend my money any way I damn well please."

"Well, thank you for stating the obvious," Constance replied. "Just make sure you know what you're doing because you just met this man, and you really don't know him. All I'm saying is watch your back and your wallet. I, on the other hand, have known you since fifth grade. I love you like a sister. I'm just looking out for you."

Her last remark seemed to simmer Tameka down. "It's cool. I don't want to fight."

"Yeah, because you know I'd win," Constance jeered. "Let's just go and have a good time."

They left the ladies' room all smiles.

The Spot was jumping. People were laughing, drinking, and having a good time. Constance made her way up to the bar to order another cranberry and vodka. A few brothas and sugar daddies approached her along the way, but she rejected each one of them with a smile. The wait at the bar was long, but she didn't care. She would have done anything to get away from Tameka and Jermaine. Those two were all hugged up, kissing, and calling each other stupid pet names like "snuggie uggie" and "pumpkin pie." It made Constance want to vomit.

She was waiting at the bar when someone placed a hand on her arm. The touch sent chills up her spine, and a familiar fragrance lingered in the air. Constance hesitantly turned around, not wanting to be disappointed. Sure enough, there stood Ahyende, tall and handsome. Constance took a moment to take him all in. He looked regal in an all-white linen suit.

"I knew it was you," he said. "I'd know you anywhere."

Constance was at a loss for words. She stood motionless as the alcohol began to take its effect. Her breaths became slow and heavy. Her chest heaved in a slow rhythm.

Ahyende stood still admiring her beauty. He analyzed every part of her, the way her hair lay, the scent of her perfume, the tiny traces of perspiration glistening on her skin.

A sultry love serenade began to play. Ahyende gave Constance his hand. "Dance with me."

Slowly, he guided her to the dance floor and pulled her close. As they swayed to the music, Ahyende let his hand slowly glide down Constance's waist, and he tightened his grasp as she looked deep into his eyes. He stroked her cheek with his thumb and pressed his lips against her ear.

Softly, he said, "I don't know what it means, but I

haven't been able to stop thinking about you since we met."

Constance closed her eyes and placed her head on Ahyende's chest. At that moment, every worry, concern, and person in that room disappeared. The world only contained the two of them. They didn't utter another word. They used their bodies to speak. A sway of the hips, a touch, a slight caress. Even their hearts began to beat in synchrony. They continued to dance, unaware that the music had switched to an upbeat mix. When they noticed they were the only two people slow dancing on the dance floor, Ahyende led Constance to a quiet booth.

"Not to sound cliché, but do you come here often?" he asked.

Constance laughed at his attempt to be cute. "I take advantage of it when I can," she replied.

"So what else is there to do in H-Town? Bull riding, cow roping, barn raising?"

"I see you're full of jokes, and not very funny ones, at that."

The two chuckled.

"But seriously, what is there to do in this city? This is the first time I've been out."

"All work and no play?" Constance said, attempting to be coy.

"Well, maybe what I need is a playmate," Ahyende cooed as he stroked her hand.

Tameka and Jermaine made their way over to the booth. "So is this where you've been hiding? I hope we aren't interrupting anything." Constance knew that Tameka was being facetious. Tameka *hoped* she was interrupting.

"Of course not." Constance tried to gain her composure. "Have a seat, you two."

Tameka slid in next to Ahyende.

"Ahyende, I'd like you to meet Tameka and her friend." Constance didn't dare introduce Jermaine as a member of her father's church.

The three exchanged pleasantries, and Tameka immediately began the interrogation. Nothing out of the ordinary, just the usual to determine six degrees of separation. "Which college did you attend? Are you Greek?"

If he failed to answer either of the simple yet pertinent questions, it could make the difference between life and social suicide.

"Why don't I order us some appetizers?" Constance intercepted.

She motioned for the server, and the group placed their orders. Tameka, however, was not done.

"You know, you look really familiar," she told Ahyende. "Have we met before?"

"No," he replied. "I'm sure I would remember that."

"Well, I'm rarely wrong about these things. What church do you attend?"

Here it comes, thought Constance.

"I haven't found a church home," Ahyende replied, somehow sensing Constance's uneasiness.

Already, they seemed to be in tune, and Constance relished in the feeling.

For the rest of the evening, the foursome enjoyed good food, music, and conversation, only leaving when the lights came on, signaling the club's close.

CHAPTER FIVE

Funny How Time Flies

*D*ays passed since Constance had seen Ahyende at The Spot. She hadn't heard from him, either. She didn't have his number, but he had hers, and he knew where she worked. It bothered her for a while because they'd had such a great time together. However, she figured that maybe he had met someone else, someone who was available, and she couldn't fault him for that. Constance reached into her nightstand, pulled out her engagement ring, and placed it on her finger.

"Oh, well," she said to herself. "The fantasy was fun while it lasted."

On her way to work, she received a call on her cell phone. She answered, hoping it was Ahyende, only to be disappointed to learn it was Antonio.

"I hope you haven't forgotten about the party," he said.

"I'm not going to be able to make it. I haven't been

feeling well," she lied. "I'm certain it's food poisoning, and I'm pulling up to the doctor's office now. Sorry again."

Constance hung up feeling renewed. She could finally have a clean start with Marvin without the ghost of Antonio lurking around.

At work, Constance was a wreck. Her head sprung with every chime of the bell, and Alicia couldn't help but notice.

"Girl, have you had your morning coffee?"

Constance looked puzzled. "What do you mean?"

"What I mean is how jumpy you are every time that damn door chimes. Are you hoping Marvin walks in and sees you wearing that ring?"

"Huh?" For a moment, Constance had forgotten she was wearing her engagement ring. "Oh, yeah." She rolled her eyes. "Is it that obvious?"

"Not as obvious as that small city you're wearing on your hand," Keith interjected. "Honey, I would wear that to my grave, okay!"

He and Alicia slapped each other five.

"Yes, it is nice." Constance was uninterested.

"Sweetie, nice is a one-carat solitaire. You have a platinum, *five*-carat, princess-cut, ten-thousand-dollar engagement ring on your hand!" Keith said, swooning.

Alicia turned to Keith. "Damn, did you go to the back and google the ring? She just wore it today, and you know its entire history."

"Sweetie, when you're as admired as moi, you get accustomed to the finer things."

"Well, that's funny because I've never seen you show up to work wearing a diamond anything," Alicia sassed.

"Well, not yet, but you just keep on watching, honey."

Their banter began to annoy Constance, so she decided to complete some paperwork in her office. She was barely in there thirty minutes before Alicia came knocking on the door.

She stuck her head in. "Hey, girl. Are you okay?" she asked.

"I'm fine."

"Oh, okay. Well, in that case, there's someone here to see you."

"Who?" Constance asked.

"I'm not sure. I didn't ask for her name. She's pregnant. That's all I know."

Other than Yvette, there was only one pregnant woman Constance could think of, and there was no way she would be there. Constance searched the floor for a familiar face, unprepared for who she saw.

"Hey, girl! How are you?" Monique was cheerful and upbeat. She reached in and gave Constance a hug.

Constance was puzzled. "What brings you by?"

"Well, I was in the neighborhood and decided to check you out. I really like your store."

"Why, thank you," Constance said through a loosely threaded smile. "Be sure to have a good look around, and let Alicia know if you need anything. I'd help you, but I have a ton of paperwork to finish."

"Oh, you're busy?" Monique asked. "I thought you

could help me pick out some jewelry to wear for the party. You're still coming, aren't you? It'll give us a chance to meet your boyfriend ..." Monique's jaw dropped at the sight of Constance's ring. "Or, should I say, fiancé? Oh, my gosh, you're engaged!" she squealed. "This is news to me. Antonio never said a word."

"It just happened recently."

"Well, congratulations!" Monique seemed sincere. "I will gladly refer you to my wedding coordinator. Have you set a date?"

Constance was beginning to feel awkward, so she changed the subject. "So many questions. Let's not think about that now. We've got to find you some jewelry."

She led Monique around the shop making sure to suggest the most expensive pieces. Monique was impressed with the boutique. She not only bought a few hundred dollars in jewelry, but she also left with two designer dresses.

As soon as she was done with Monique, Constance bolted for the door. The early morning call from Antonio and pop-up visit from his wife were a little too much for her. She had to indulge in an afternoon drink.

Nothing like this ever happened to me before I put this ring on my hand, she thought.

She parked her car and entered her favorite Mexican restaurant. No sooner had she been shown her seat did she look up and see Mrs. Wallace, who had already spotted her and was making her way to the table. Constance hadn't seen her since the surprise proposal; however, she had sent her flowers.

"Well, good afternoon, Constance. Imagine my surprise seeing you here." Mrs. Wallace was curt per usual.

Constance never felt comfortable talking to her. She felt Marvin's mother scrutinized every word.

"I come here often. They have great lunch specials. However, I wouldn't take this as your sort of place," Constance said.

"Oh, goodness, no. One of my Links sisters suggested we meet here to discuss chapter business. She swears by their margaritas. I decided it wouldn't kill me to try something new. I would assume you agree. I see you're trying something new, too."

"I beg your pardon?"

"I'm speaking of you wearing your ring, dear, or have you forgotten that you're wearing it? I don't see how that could be; it *is* heavy enough, isn't it?"

Constance was flabbergasted. The server came to the table to take her order, and Mrs. Wallace took that as her cue to leave.

"Well, it was good to see you, dear. You and I have to get together some time, just the two of us. Take care."

Constance was at a loss for words. She tried to enjoy her meal, but Mrs. Wallace's remarks had spoiled her appetite. And she couldn't stop thinking about Ahyende, wondering why he still hadn't called. No sooner had she thought about him did her cell phone ring.

"Hello, Constance. It's Monique."

Twice in one day? She could not get rid of this chick.

"I hope you don't mind. I got your number from

Antonio. He told me you said you were ill and couldn't make it to the party. What's going on? Did I do something to offend you?"

Constance wanted to tell her, "Yes, you did something to offend me. You stole my soulmate, you're living the life I'm supposed to live, and the fact that you are such a nice, sweet, trusting person makes me even angrier, and I want to punch you," but she knew that wouldn't be the right thing to do.

"No, you didn't do anything. I am embarrassed to tell you this, but I haven't had the time to get a gift, and I didn't want to show up empty handed."

"Just bring yourself and that fiancé. All the food is taken care of. I'm sure you would have gotten something if you had the time. You're a busy business woman. Your day is filled with taking care of your boutique."

Monique had twisted her arm. "Well, I guess I'll see you Saturday."

"Great. I can't wait to give you a tour of the place."

It's too late for that.

The day of Antonio's birthday party had come. Constance thought it would be best not to invite Tameka after she'd practically admonished her about Jermaine. Instead, she invited Marvin and, oddly enough, he accepted. It seemed he was eager to go anywhere with her since she'd started wearing her engagement ring.

He was impressed as they drove up to Antonio's

waterfront home. "Well, so far it seems these friends have class," he commented.

Constance held her tongue. The valet greeted them as they pulled up front.

Marvin seemed pleased. "I think these are definitely our type of people." He took Constance's hand and headed up the steps to the front door.

She took a deep breath and said a silent prayer as they entered the home.

The entryway was remarkable, and the home was impeccable, with high ceilings, marble floors, and a spiral staircase. Constance felt a pang of jealousy in the pit of her stomach. She looked to Marvin, who was beaming, admiring all the fine artisanship of the home.

He whispered to her, "We have got to find out who their realtor was."

Antonio and Monique stood amongst a sea of guests as they entered the foyer. His arms were wrapped lovingly around his wife.

"Is that them?" Marvin asked, motioning toward the couple.

"That's them."

"Well, let's let them know we're here." Marvin was quite eager.

Reluctantly, she approached their hosts. Antonio's eyes lit up the moment he saw Constance standing before him in her red bandage dress. She had purposely worn it to make him salivate, and she could see that it was working. Monique and Antonio greeted her with a big hug.

"I'm so glad you made it," said Monique. "And this must be your fiancé!"

"Hello, I'm Marvin. It is a pleasure to meet you both."

The vibrato in his voice made him sound as if he were on an interview. The entire situation began to make Constance uneasy. She reached for a glass of champagne as the server passed and consumed it quickly. Marvin was embarrassed and threw her a glare.

As Constance surveyed the room, she noticed many familiar faces, but none of whom she cared to remember. She was beginning to regret not inviting Tameka after all. At least she would've had someone to talk to.

Marvin found his way to a far corner, holding a conversation with a bunch of men she could correctly assume were his frat brothers because of the way they all kept shouting "Yo!" Marvin could find a frat brother at any social function.

The hours crept by, and Constance's third glass of champagne was beginning to kick in, making her feel euphoric. She surveyed the room for Marvin but couldn't recall where she had seen him last. "Bastard," she mumbled to no one in particular. "How dare he agree to come and then ditch me?"

She began searching for him, going from room to room. Each room on the ground floor was filled with guests. She was making her way down a hall when she bumped into Antonio.

"Hey, boo-boo. You having a good time?"

"Hardly," she retorted, trying to pass.

"Hold up, baby. What's the rush?"

"I'm looking for my fiancé."

Antonio chuckled. "I've been meaning to ask you about that. When were you going to tell me about your engagement?"

"Never, which is about the same amount of time it took you to tell me about yours."

Antonio rolled his eyes. "Oh, here we go. You're never going to let me live that down, are you?"

"Live down what, the fact that I had to hear from everyone I knew but you that you were engaged? At least you can say you heard it from me first."

"No, I didn't hear it from you. I had to hear it from my wife."

"Exactly, your *wife*. You're married to Monique and about to have a baby. Why do you care what I do?"

"Because we're soulmates. We just got caught up in other stuff and lost focus on each other."

Antonio had Constance backed against the wall. He smelled so good, and he looked good, too. He was dressed in nothing more than a simple button-down shirt, jeans, and boots. His jewelry, however, set off the outfit. He wore a platinum chain and a Rolex that shone so brightly she thought she needed sunglasses to look at him. The tattoos on his neck peeked from underneath his collar. With all his money and success, Antonio still held traces of the 'hood he'd left behind. His rough exterior turned her on. As he moved in closer, she could feel his breath on her face.

"That dude with the stuffy suit ain't the one for you, baby. You like your men the way you like to get fucked—hard and rough. That daddy's girl image may work on him, but it never worked on me."

He was so close that Constance could feel his bulging erection through his pants. Antonio slid his hand up her dress and onto her thigh. He cupped her ass with one hand and placed the other between her legs as he began to massage her clit. Although she knew she should, Constance didn't stop him. Just one touch from Antonio made her wetter than the Amazon.

"I see I'm not the only one who wants this. Come on, tell me you want it."

She shook her head.

He put more pressure on her clit. "Tell me you want it," he commanded as he began to caress her nipples through her dress.

"I want it," she whispered, surprised by her own response.

Antonio kissed Constance so passionately, she forgot they were in the hallway. The gravity of the situation quickly sank in. She pulled away from Antonio and slapped his face.

"Damn, baby! You still got it!" he raved, even more turned on.

"Are you crazy? We are at a party in your house. We both have far too much to lose."

"Please," he replied. "This ain't Monique's first rodeo.

What, she thought trapping me with a kid was gonna make me change?"

Constance couldn't believe her ears. His words filled her with disgust. "You know what, Antonio, you're a real piece of shit. Erase my number and forget you ever knew me." Constance adjusted her dress and continued her search to find Marvin, but Antonio wasn't about to let her go that easily.

"Calm down. After all this time, you finally decide to grow a conscience?"

"Well, at least one of us has," she spat. "I'm done being your sure thing. No, Marvin may not have your swagger, but he's bright, he's ambitious, and he has a promising future."

Antonio laughed.

"What's so funny?"

"You never mentioned anything about love."

"Love? Please, love is for the delusional. Monique loves you, and all she got was a nice home and a cheating husband." With those words, she stormed off.

Constance checked the kitchen one last time for Marvin, only to find Monique.

"Hey, girl. Where have you been?" Monique asked.

"I'm looking for my fiancé. Have you seen him?"

"He's down in the game room. I was just about to take some more hors d'oeuvres down there."

Constance followed Monique to the game room and found Marvin at the bar drinking tequila shots and smoking a cigar.

"Where have you been?" Constance asked. "I've been looking for you all over the house."

"Well, you found me. So what do you want?" Marvin's eyes were glossy, and his speech was slurred.

"I'm ready to go and, by the looks of things, so are you."

Marvin turned to Constance with a puzzled look. "I'll tell you when I'm ready to go. Now, either go mingle or sit in the car and wait until I'm ready."

The other men in the room grew quiet.

Constance was embarrassed. "Fine. Can I have the keys, please?"

Marvin released a deep breath. "Go get the keys from the valet and sit in the car, if that will get you to shut the hell up."

Marvin was a snide person normally, but he was a mean drunk. Constance quickly left, but Monique stopped her on the way out.

"You're leaving so soon?"

"I have to get up pretty early tomorrow."

Monique looked disappointed. "I wanted to show you the baby's nursery before you left."

"Maybe next time. Goodnight."

"Okay then. How about I give you a call soon, and we can have lunch?"

Oh, my God. This girl just will not give up. "Sure, you do that."

Constance let herself out and waited for the car to come around. She tipped the valet, got into the car, and drove off. She knew Marvin would be pissed, but she didn't care. *Let him catch a ride home with his newfound friends,* she thought as she headed home. This was a night she wanted to forget.

It was well past midnight when Constance's doorbell rang. She opened the door to find Marvin standing there with a man she recognized from Antonio's party.

"Thanks for walking me up, Nupe. I'm at the right place." Marvin gave the man their fraternal handshake and made his way into Constance's condo.

He didn't say one word or even look at her. He simply kicked off his shoes and collapsed on the sofa. Constance got a blanket from the hall closet and placed it over him. She returned to her bed and checked her call log one last time before she closed her eyes and drifted off to sleep.

CHAPTER SIX

What Goes Around . . .

*I*t was past noon when Constance was awakened by her chiming cell phone. She had missed calls and text messages from both Yvette and Tameka, wondering why she wasn't at Sunday service. She quickly texted a reply, asking them to meet her for brunch. She rose to take a shower but remembered she had to get rid of Marvin. His behavior last night did not sit well with her, and she wanted to confront him.

Constance went downstairs, expecting to rile Marvin from an alcohol-induced slumber, only to find an empty sofa and a tossed blanket. She checked the downstairs half-bath, thinking maybe he had fallen asleep with his head in the toilet. She found nothing, not even a note saying he had left. She searched the living room for clues as to where he could have gone. The only evidence she found was an unlocked deadbolt. Marvin hadn't left his wallet, so she knew he wasn't coming back. She returned upstairs to change for brunch, determined not to let him ruin yet another day.

It wasn't long before she was dressed and on her way to meet her besties at Kulture. The drive was short, but the entire way there, Constance had the strangest feeling she was being followed. She was a cautious driver and persistently checked her rearview mirror. It wasn't until her third check in the mirror that she took notice of a black sedan. It stopped at every light and made every turn she made.

"Come on, Connie, don't get paranoid," she said to herself. "Maybe they're going to the restaurant, too. After all, it is a public place."

Constance made a right at the last light before the restaurant and checked her rearview mirror. Again, she noticed the sedan, but the driver kept straight ahead. Constance shook her head and laughed at her paranoia as she pulled up to the valet. Yvette and Tameka were already seated when she arrived.

"Looks like you and Marvin pulled an all-nighter," Tameka teased.

"Hardly," Constance replied.

She told her friends how Antonio had accosted her but intentionally left out the details of Marvin's behavior.

Yvette showed no emotion as she listened to the previous night's events, while Tameka hung on to Constance's every word, adding in her two cents wherever she saw fit.

"Girl, you're crazy. I would've given Antonio a little taste. That is one fine, sexy man," Tameka said.

"But he's married," Yvette added. "Connie, you didn't do anything, did you?"

Constance kept silent.

"Did you, Connie?" she asked again.

Constance replied slowly. "I ... We sort of kissed."

"Girl, you are scandalous!" replied Tameka gleefully. "Was it a good kiss? Did he make you weak in the knees?"

Ashamed, Constance placed her head in her hand.

Yvette was beside herself. "Connie, I can't believe you. Marriage vows are sacred and not something to be taken lightly."

Tameka had heard enough. "Take it easy, Mother Teresa. He knows he's married. It's not like she chased him. He pursued *her*."

"But that doesn't change the facts, and the fact is he is a married man." Yvette's voice was beginning to carry, and a few of the other restaurant patrons turned in her direction.

"Yes, Yvette, we all know that he's married, and now, so does half the restaurant," Constance chided.

"What's gotten into you, girl," asked Tameka. "You're kissing Antonio, and that island man from The Spot is all up in church asking me if I've seen you."

Constance choked on her water. "You saw Ahyende?"

"Ah-who?" Yvette asked.

Tameka gave a sly grin. "Oh, so I know something you don't know?" She looked at Constance. "Our good friend,

Connie, befriended the visitor from church and met up with him the other night at The Spot."

"Tameka, that is a lie," Constance snapped.

"So, it was pure coincidence that you met up there?"

"Yes. He's new to the city and went out to see what the city's nightlife was like."

"My, my ... How do you know so much about someone you just happened to bump into?" Tameka asked.

Constance was losing her patience. "Can we just order, please? Where is our waiter?"

"Connie, why are you getting so defensive?" Tameka asked.

"I'm not getting defensive, Tameka. I have yet to be seen by a waiter. I'm starving. I haven't eaten breakfast, and you know how I get when I'm hungry."

Within seconds, the waiter came to their table, and Constance couldn't be more pleased.

"Well," added Tameka, "he gave me his business card to give you, but if you like, I can keep it for myself."

Constance tried to conceal her excitement, but she didn't hesitate to free the card from Tameka's grasp.

"I'll take it," she said as she quickly retrieved the business card from Tameka's clutches. "He knows I'm part of the new members' ministry," she lied. "He probably just has some questions in case he decides to join the church."

"Connie, I hope you're right," Yvette said. "I know you and Marvin have had your issues, but you're engaged now, and you seem happy. I hope you think this through."

"There is nothing to think about," Constance assured

her. "I *am* happily engaged to Marvin. Did the two of you not notice that I'm wearing my engagement ring?"

"Finally," Tameka uttered under her breath.

Constance rolled her eyes.

Their food arrived, and they dropped the conversation to enjoy their brunch. Constance played it cool but, inside, she was celebrating. It seemed Ahyende was thinking of her just as she had been thinking of him. As she dined on eggs benedict, the only thing Constance could think of was calling Ahyende.

The trio finished brunch faster than the time it took them to have their conversation, and by the end of the meal, everyone's tempers had calmed. The friends parted ways for the day, each one promising to call the other. It took the valet quite some time to bring Constance's car around. She stood alone waiting before she decided to ask about the delay.

Finally, the valet arrived, but without her car. "Excuse me, ma'am," said the young valet, "but there seems to be a problem with your car."

"A problem? What sort of problem?"

"Let me get my manager, and we can walk around to your vehicle together."

Constance complied with the young man, but she was curious as to what this "problem" may be.

A considerable amount of time passed before the valet returned with the manager, who looked concerned. "Hello, ma'am. I'm Peter Lee, the manager of this establishment.

Could you come into my office, please, so we may discuss the issue in private?"

Constance was agitated. "No, we cannot!" she spat. "We can discuss the issue right here!"

"Ma'am, please. It seems to be a delicate matter. I would prefer to discuss this in private."

"And I would prefer that you tell me, now, what the problem is, or else bring my car around."

"Well, that's just it, ma'am. We can't bring your car around," Peter answered.

"Why? Was it stolen?"

"No, ma'am. I can assure you that your vehicle was not stolen."

"So, what is the problem?"

Peter took a deep breath. "The problem is that it's on flat."

Constance was puzzled and relieved. "Well, that's not a problem. I know how to fix a flat."

"No, ma'am. You don't understand. All four tires are flat—slashed."

"There must be some mistake. Are you positive it's my car? On second thought, let me check for myself."

Constance went to the valet lot and couldn't believe her eyes. Not only was her car sitting on four flat tires, but the word WHORE was keyed into the hood. A range of emotions rushed through her blood. Immediately, she blamed the valets.

"How incompetent is your staff! You didn't see who did this to my car?"

The young valet stood in silence.

"What were you doing while my car was being vandalized?" she screeched.

"Ma'am, please," Peter interjected. "We will get to the bottom of this. Let us take care of your meal."

"My *meal*? If you think paying for a sixty-dollar brunch is equivalent to my eighty-thousand-dollar car, then you're even more incompetent than these adolescents you've hired as valets!"

"Please, there is no need for belligerence. We will call the police, and you can file a report."

"No, that is *not* good enough. I want to see the surveillance tape."

Peter's head hung low. "I'm sorry, but that isn't possible. You see, last night we experienced a break in, and all of our surveillance equipment was taken."

Constance laughed hysterically. "Of course, your equipment is gone. How foolish of me to think that a four-star restaurant would have something as simple as security cameras! I hope you have insurance, because you will definitely be hearing from my lawyer."

Constance took out her cell phone and called Marvin.

"Marvin, baby, I'm having an issue with my car. Could you please come get me?"

Marvin let out a groan. "Baby, I'm so hungover. Can't you call anyone else?"

"Marvin, I need you. My car has been completely vandalized, and my parents are away on church business. You're the only person who can come get me."

Marvin let out a sigh. "I wish I could, but I'm sick as a dog, and I have a huge deposition in the morning. What about those friends of yours? Can't you get one of them to do it?"

"Marvin, *you're* my man, not my friends. As my future husband, it's your obligation to help me when I need you."

"Look, it's either their help or no help. It doesn't feel good to be left stranded, does it?" He hung up.

Tears began to well in her eyes as she placed a call to nine-one-one. The police report was solely for insurance purposes. Constance knew that, legally, without a surveillance video, not much could be done.

The officer asked her the usual questions like if she had any enemies or a jealous ex. They even questioned the valets. No one had seen or heard anything. The only thing Constance could do was go home and wait. She had the car towed to a body shop and, fortunately, the tow truck driver was kind enough to give her a ride home.

Back home, she couldn't shake what happened at the restaurant. She was too afraid to stay home alone. She thought about staying at her parents' house, but they were still away. The news about her car would only worry Yvette, which would make Constance worry even more. So she packed a bag and decided to call and ask Tameka to come get her.

She fumbled through her purse with shaky fingers, searching for her cell phone. She pushed back her makeup bag to discover Ahyende's business card.

Should I call him? If anything, it'll take my mind off

75

this drama. It's not as if my fiancé is worried about me. She decided to call Ahyende, her heart pounding with every dial tone.

The phone rang a few times before he picked up. "Ahyende speaking." His voice was as smooth as velvet.

Constance's brain drew a blank. Her palms began to sweat, and she almost hung up, but Ahyende's voice drew her back in.

"Hello, is anyone there?" he asked.

Constance cleared her throat. "Hello, Ahyende. It's Constance McGuire."

"Constance, hi. I was hoping you would call."

"Yeah, I was bored and decided to give you a call. Wait, that didn't sound very nice. I was ..." She was flustered as she searched for the right words. Ahyende's voice had her heart pounding, and the car vandal still had her nerves on edge.

"Constance, are you okay?" he asked.

With those words, he had done what Marvin had not, and Constance found herself at ease. Without hesitation, she informed Ahyende of the incident with her car, even sharing how Marvin refused to help. Ahyende listened attentively without interruption.

"Where do you live? I'm coming over."

Constance was shocked. "No, you don't have to do that. I've planned on staying with a friend."

"Constance, you can't let this person bully you out of your home. Besides, this could just be some strange case of mistaken identity. You can't let this creep win. My offer to come over still stands. I can just come over to keep you company and ease your mind."

He had a point. She did still feel cautious, and she knew she would feel better having a man by her side for protection, especially one as fine as Ahyende, so she accepted his offer.

Constance got off the phone and looked at herself in the mirror. She looked a complete mess. Her face was pale and her hair was disheveled. There was no way she could allow Ahyende to see her in such a state. She quickly went upstairs to wash away the grit and grime of the day. It took her minutes to change into a comfortable white cotton tee and a pair of yoga pants. She quickly flat ironed her hair and dabbed on her favorite perfume. The only thing left to do was make hors d'oeuvres and wait for Ahyende.

CHAPTER SEVEN

... Comes Around

Constance's doorbell rang, and she gave herself one last look in the mirror before opening the door. There stood Ahyende looking exquisite in a simple white tee, jeans, and construction boots. The crisp white color of the t-shirt was a perfect complement to his coal-black skin. He sported a boyish grin and held a bouquet of tulips. His simple yet thoughtful gesture flattered Constance, and she could feel her cheeks begin to flush.

"Thank you," she said, taking the flowers. "Tulips are my favorite. Please, come in."

Ahyende's body brushed against hers as he passed the threshold, and his slight touch gave her butterflies. Constance had to shake the feeling. No matter how much of a jerk Marvin had been, she had taken the first step to the ultimate commitment and was determined to see it through.

"You have a very nice place," Ahyende said. "Did you decorate it yourself?"

"Yes, I did. It's a hobby of mine," Constance said with words that seemed too rushed. "Please, have a seat on the sofa. I made a few hors d'oeuvres. It's not much, just a few meats, olives, and cheeses I threw together. They're on the table. Help yourself."

Ahyende sat comfortably on the sofa, soaking in the ambiance. The fragrances of sandalwood and lavender filled the air as oils and incense burned.

"Would you like a glass of wine?" Constance asked from the kitchen. "I have red and white."

"I'll take whatever you're having," Ahyende replied.

Constance emerged from the kitchen with two wine glasses and a bottle of her best Sauvignon Blanc. It had been years since Constance had entertained a man other than Marvin, and she wasn't sure of what the two of them should do; however, all Ahyende wanted to do was talk about her. He asked questions about her childhood, her family, interests, career, and she, in turn, asked him the same. Ahyende educated Constance on his childhood in Trinidad. He spoke of his homeland with passion and adoration. He described each memory with vivid and candid detail, his words dripping from his lips like the juices from a honeydew melon.

Constance was enamored with the man seated beside her. She let out a sensual sigh. "You make it sound like a paradise," she said.

79

"Oh, my dear, but it is. You have to visit some time. I'll be your personal tour guide if you like."

"I'd like that very much," Constance said, running her fingers through her hair.

"Forgive me if I'm being rude, but I have never met a black woman with auburn hair. Green eyes, yes, but never red hair. It is unique. Yes, Miss McGuire, you are a rare beauty, indeed."

Ahyende's words hung in the air. The pair locked eyes as they inched closer to each other, their hearts pounding through their chests. It was as if a magnet were pulling them toward each other. There was no thought, no hesitation, before the two found themselves engaged in a passionate kiss. Ahyende's lips were lava against Constance's skin. He pulled her head back gently as he kissed her neck, moving closer to her breasts. His hands lovingly caressed the curves of her body, making her feel safe and wanted. Waves of emotion rushed over Constance as she mounted Ahyende and removed his shirt, her fingers racing across his rippled stomach and chiseled chest. Ahyende lifted her top to view her voluptuous breasts heaving heavily with desire. He removed her bra and placed her breasts in each of his hands, suckling her erect nipples, burying his face into her cleavage. Constance slid her hands down Ahyende's pants, massaging his massive erection. He moaned as she gave his shaft a firm grasp. It had been some time since she felt like this. All logical thinking had gone out the window.

He paused suddenly. "Wait, Constance. We can't do this."

Constance snapped out of her lust-induced trance. She was puzzled. "Why not? I know you feel what I feel. We can't continue to ignore it."

"I agree," he said. "But we also can't continue to ignore the fact that you are in a relationship with someone else. This is not how I want you. When I give myself to you, I want it to be freely and without regrets. I want to know that no one else dwells in your walls but me. This may sound crazy, and I have only known you a few weeks, but I'm falling in love with you. For me to make love to you would only confirm what I'm feeling. I want you, but not like this."

Constance quickly sat up and put on her t-shirt. "I haven't been able to stop thinking about you since the day I saw you in church. I feel so close to you, so connected, but I'm not willing to give up something I've had for the past seven years. I barely know you."

"And yet you're willing to sleep with me? Constance, you're making yourself sound like a whore."

Constance was insulted. "How dare you? I am *not* a whore!"

"Then prove it and be with me. This person left you stranded at a restaurant under dire circumstances, and you think that's love? I would never do that to you. To me, you're regal, and I would do anything and everything in my power to treat you as such. I know how you feel about me. I can see it in your eyes. I know because it's the same way I look at you. I'm not in this for sex; I want you, all of you, not just your body. Constance, I want your heart."

Constance sat bewildered and confused. She had waited so long for a man to say those words to her, but she had always hoped that man would be Marvin. "I don't know what to do. I don't know if I can be as certain as you are. We barely know each other. How do I know the feelings I have for you won't pass?"

"Your feelings won't pass because I will do everything I can to make you feel the way you felt that day at the coffee house."

Constance became overwhelmed with emotion. A single tear rolled down her cheek and plummeted onto her lap.

Ahyende held her close. "I know you're scared. Hell, I'm scared, too, but I am a man of my word, and I told you that I will wait for you. Constance, sometimes you just have to step out on faith. You can't let your head do all the thinking for you. You've gotta listen to your heart sometimes, too."

They held each other in silence until they fell asleep.

The following weeks were filled with secret lunches and secluded phone calls from Ahyende. Constance would leave the boutique to meet him for coffee or lunch. They always engaged in stimulating conversation and hand-holding but never anything sexual. Ahyende was a man of his word.

Lately, it had become more difficult to conceal the clandestine love affair, but that didn't stop them from seeing each other. Constance longed for Ahyende with each passing day and grew less interested in Marvin. Not much changed between them. He still showed little to no interest in helping find the person who had vandalized her car, and he became increasingly unavailable. The two occasionally engaged in monotonous sex; however, he went from canceling dinner plans and dates with Constance to not making them at all. She didn't mind, necessarily, because it gave her more time to be with Ahyende, but she would be lying if she said she didn't feel a little neglected. The only time he really saw her was to show her off at dinners with clients or company events. He would arrive at her door with a smile and some new gaudy piece of jewelry and instruct her to wear it. One night, it was a sapphire necklace, the next, a pair of diamond earrings. She admired the gifts, but she also knew they came with a price. Marvin would parade her around a room, showing her off with all the ornamentation while he watched other men salivate over his most prized possession. He was quite haughty whenever someone commented on Constance's stunning beauty. She would just smile meekly and say, "Thank you." Marvin didn't like for her to talk too much around the partners. He always said that an outspoken woman made a man appear weak. He claimed that a man in his profession couldn't afford to seem weak because it would ruin him and everything he was working so hard for.

Marvin would spend the evening schmoozing, while she danced with his colleagues. For the most part, they were respectful, of course. They had to be with their wives there, but there was always the one who thought his money and prestige could get him whatever he wanted. In those circumstances, Constance would just laugh and bat her emerald beauties. "I'm sorry," she'd say, "but I'm taken. However, if that ever changes, you'll be the first person I call." The slimy suckers fell for the line every time. And as she swayed to the sounds of some big jazz band, her mind drifted to thoughts of Ahyende.

CHAPTER EIGHT

When It Rains It Pours

Weeks passed, and things were beginning to look up for Constance. Although there was still no word on her car vandal, her vehicle was repaired, business was booming, and she had plans to expand and open a second location. Although she and Marvin had yet to set a wedding date, her bond with Ahyende grew stronger. And while their affair was still very much a secret, she didn't know how long she could keep it that way. Ahyende was growing weary of having to keep his affection for her concealed. A few times, he showed up to her job unannounced, which piqued Alicia's curiosity. Just yesterday, while out for coffee, he'd leaned over and kissed her on the mouth in front of everyone. Constance was taken aback; however, she did nothing to stop him. She knew she had to talk to him about his behavior immediately and figured she would do it today over lunch.

Constance was busy with her day at the boutique when she received a call from Yvette.

"Connie, it's time," Yvette said through heavy breaths.

"It's time? I can't believe it! It's time!" Constance jumped up and down frantically. "Alicia, I have to go. It's time!"

She ran to the office to grab her purse and dashed to the door. She called Tameka on her way to the hospital and, as always, got her voicemail. She left a message and instructed Tameka to meet her at the hospital immediately. The normal forty-five-minute drive to the women's hospital took her just twenty. Constance raced to Labor and Delivery to find her friend. The nurses were busy reading monitors and taking Yvette's blood pressure when Constance barged in.

"Hey, girl. How are you feeling? Are you nervous? Do you need some ice chips or another pillow? Nurse, another pillow, please."

"I'm fine." Yvette laughed. "And I do not need another pillow. What I do need, however, is for you to calm down. I don't know who is more nervous, you or Steve."

Constance surveyed the room. "Where is Steve?"

"He stepped out to have a cigarette."

"Since when does Steve smoke?" Constance asked.

"Since I went into labor about twelve hours ago."

"Twelve hours! When you called you said it was time."

"Well, that's what I thought, too, but it seems little Marie has her mind set on staying in there."

"Marie? That's my middle name," Constance said.

"I know. I thought it would be nice if my daughter were named after her godmother."

"Godmother!" Constance began to cry. "I promise I won't let you and Steve down," she said as she gave Yvette a hug.

"Now, stop all that crying," Yvette commanded. "You know I can't stand to see people cry," she said as she, too, began to weep.

Steve walked into the room and saw the spectacle of the two women hugging as they shared tears of joy.

"I guess she knows she's the godmother," he said.

The three of them laughed.

"Have you called Tameka?" Yvette asked. "I want her to be here, too."

"Yes, I called," said Constance, "but, as always, I had to leave a message. But don't worry, you know she'll be here."

Two hours passed and there was still no change in the baby's position nor had Tameka made an appearance. The doctor came in to examine Yvette's progress (or lack thereof) and drew a look of concern. "It looks like we're going to have to prep you for a C-section," he said.

"Are you sure?" Steve asked.

"Positive. With every passing hour, Yvette's blood pressure is dropping, and that's not good for her or the baby. You can go in," he said to Steve, "but you, ma'am, have to wait in the lobby," he told Constance. "I'll be back in fifteen minutes."

"A C-section?" Yvette cried. "I'm not prepared for this.

I waited too long to have another baby. This is not the way it's supposed to be. Mothers are supposed to push their children into the world not have them cut out."

Constance and Steve tried their best to console her.

"Yvette, listen to me," said Constance. "You have cared for and nurtured that baby for the past nine months. You've done your job. Now, let the doctors do theirs."

"She's right, honey," Steve said.

"I can't lose another baby," Yvette sobbed.

"And we won't. We have the Almighty God here in this room with us, and when we go into the surgical room, He will be in there, too. Your only job right now is to relax and have faith that He will give you strength and see this through." Steve held his wife's hand and gently kissed her on the lips.

Constance longed for what they had. She turned her back to wipe the tears streaming down her face.

"Guys," she said. "I'd like to take this time to pray before the doctor comes back into the room."

The three of them joined hands as Constance led them in prayer.

"Father God, we come to You as humbly as we know how. We come to You with our hearts filled with love and concern for the health of Yvette and Baby Marie. We ask, Dear Heavenly Father, that the Holy Spirit moves in that surgical room and guides the doctor's hands, Dear God. We ask that Your angels surround Yvette and Marie and no harm will come to them. And we ask that, with all Your wonderful and awesome power, Oh Mighty Father, when all is done, we will behold Steve and Yvette's beautiful, healthy, baby girl in her mother's arms. In Your Son Jesus's name, we do pray. Amen."

"Amen," Yvette and Steve said simultaneously.

No one noticed a nurse who had come in and was standing by the door. "Excuse me," she said. "I'm not a religious person, but that was beautiful."

"She's anointed," Yvette replied. "Now, let's go have us a baby."

Another hour passed before Tameka arrived carrying a huge bouquet of balloons and flowers. "I'm here! Where's the baby?" she shouted.

"Yvette is in surgery. She had to have a cesarean," Constance explained.

"Is she okay?"

"It looks like we're about to find out," Constance replied as she noticed Steve making his way down the hall.

"She's beautiful!" he exclaimed, gleaming. "We have a healthy eight-pound, five-ounce baby girl." He turned to Constance. "And, Godmother, as soon as they bring her out, you can hold her. Today is the happiest day of my life!" he shouted as he went running down the hall.

"Godmother?" Tameka asked.

Constance sighed. "MeMe, don't start. It's nothing personal."

"That's easy for you to say, Miss Maid of Honor-slash-Godmother-slash-Favorite Friend. I don't even know why I wasted my time coming up here."

"Wasted your time? MeMe, our best friend just had a

baby, and you don't know why you're here? This isn't about me, okay? This is about Yvette and Steve and the blessing that has been bestowed upon them after their tragic loss, or did you forget about that?"

Tameka sucked her teeth. "No."

"Well then, let's be here to support them and leave all pettiness aside."

"Whatever," she replied, rolling her eyes. "Look, I need to sign this card before she gets up here. What's the baby's name?"

"Marie," Constance boasted.

"Oh, you have *got* to be fucking kidding me! I mean, could Yvette be any further up your ass? The baby has to have your name, too? I knew she never really liked me. She is always looking down on me because I'm not as holy as her or a preacher's kid like you. This is complete bullshit!"

"Will you lower your voice," Constance chided. "This is a hospital, and you need to carry yourself with some decorum."

"Oh, you're one to talk about decorum. Tell me, have you told Marvin about that island man yet?"

Constance was puzzled. "Tameka, what are you talking about?"

She released a sinister laugh. "You know damn well what I'm talking about."

"Well, I would know if there was anything to tell but, unfortunately, there isn't," Constance lied.

"Really? Listen, Connie, that good-girl crap may work on Marvin, but you're not pulling anything over on me."

"Enough with the accusations. I've already told you I don't know him. The only time I see him is at church."

"And when you're out for coffee," Tameka jeered.

Constance's face lost its color.

"I can see I struck a nerve," she added. "Now tell me this, Miss McGuire, why would an engaged woman with so much 'decorum' be seen out in public locking lips with a man that isn't her fiancé?"

Constance's face went from pale to red. Tameka had definitely stricken a nerve. "Like I said, I don't know what you're talking about," she said through clenched teeth.

There was one thing Constance had learned through the years of her father's infidelity: deny, deny, deny. If you weren't caught in the act, it never happened.

The sound of Yvette's gurney wheeling down the hallway interrupted the heated discussion.

"Well, I guess I was wrong," Tameka said. "Maybe the apple *does* fall far from the tree."

"You better watch yourself, MeMe, and the things that come out of your mouth. My father has nothing to do with this."

"Well, tell your father to stop spreading his business all through the church. Jermaine has given me more than an earful about Pastor Gerald McGuire and the things he's been up to."

Constance was fuming. "Maybe you should pay less attention to my daddy and more attention to the contents of your wallet. You took your little usher out shopping lately?"

"Oh, please. I've moved on from Jermaine. I got a new man, now, one who is fine, rich, and knows how to give it to me. I'll have to let you meet him some time. I'm sure you'll be impressed with this one."

"I'm sure I won't," Constance snapped as Yvette was rolled beside them.

Yvette was pleased to see Tameka standing there waiting on her. "MeMe, I'm so glad you're here!"

"Now, you know I wouldn't miss the birth of my best friend's only child," she said.

Constance simply shook her head in awe of how fast Tameka could flip from friend to foe. But that was the way it had always been. Since they were kids, if Constance made Tameka mad, she would retaliate with a vengeance. In high school, a boy that Tameka liked had asked Constance to prom instead of her, so Tameka started a rumor that Constance was pregnant and gave the baby away to a church member. But, as always, she came back crying and apologizing to Constance after realizing she was her only true friend. All the other girls in school were either scared of Tameka, hated her, or jumped her because of her deceitful ways. It was the way their friendship had always been. And Constance remained loyal to Tameka through thick and thin.

For the rest of the evening, Constance couldn't shake the thought of Tameka seeing her kiss Ahyende. What if she told Marvin? What if she'd snapped a picture of them as evidence? It certainly wouldn't be out of her character to be so devious. Constance had a choice to make, and she finally knew what she had to do.

Ahyende was surprised to see Constance standing on the opposite side of his door looking stunning in a simple black wrap dress and cobalt blue pumps.

"One day, I'm going to have to give you a key, so you can come in any time," he said, wearing a huge grin.

Constance didn't smile back. "Ahyende, we have to talk," she said with no emotion.

His smile quickly faded. "Is everything okay? You look worried."

"No, everything is not okay," Constance replied as she quickly passed Ahyende and sat on his sofa. "Tameka saw us kiss the other day at the coffee shop."

Now, Ahyende understood her concern. "Are you sure?"

"One hundred percent. She made it a point to let me know she'd seen us."

Ahyende's face grew long. "So, what are you going to do?" he asked.

"There's only one thing for me to do …"

Ahyende took a deep breath and a hard swallow as he prepared himself to hear the worst.

"I'm going to tell Marvin I can't marry him, not now and not ever."

Ahyende's mournful expression morphed into shock.

"I love you, Ahyende. I can no longer deny what I

know and feel. There's not a moment that goes by that I don't think about you. Every time my phone rings, I'm hoping it's you. And every night before I go to bed, I make sure to say a prayer for you. Ahyende, never in my life have I felt for a man the way I feel for you. I can't continue to be afraid. You and me together ... It just feels right, and it has felt this way from day one."

"You have no idea how happy I am to hear you say that, and I promise you'll never regret loving me."

Ahyende kissed Constance passionately, and she welcomed his embrace, unleashing months of sexual tension. He ran his hands through her hair as he placed tantalizing kisses on her neck. Each kiss sent a sensation of delight down her spine. Slowly, he navigated his way over her clavicle and moved strategically to her breasts, releasing them from her dress, exposing her erect nipples. Ahyende ran his tongue around her areola before he placed her nipple between his teeth and gave a slight tug. The overwhelming sensation of both pleasure and pain excited Constance, causing her to become warm and moist. She opened her legs slightly and welcomed the pressure Ahyende placed on her clitoris. His touch was firm yet gentle. He massaged her clit in a circular motion as he gradually increased speed and applied pressure. Constance's body trembled as her pleasure rose.

They kissed more passionately than before. The intensity had become too much for her. With a shudder, she exploded, releasing an orgasm that soaked through her panties and dress.

Ahyende smiled, quite pleased with her body's re-action to his touch. He removed his hand from between her thighs, exposing his fingertips drenched in her essence. She took Ahyende's hand and began to suck his love-drenched fingers one by one. The sight of Constance devouring her own juices hardened his bulging erection. Ahyende scooped Constance from his sofa and carried her to his bedroom. He placed her down gently and looked deeply into her eyes before he asked, "Are you sure you're ready for this?"

"I've been ready," she purred.

Ahyende lifted his crisp t-shirt. His chiseled body looked exquisite against the moonlight. Slowly, he removed his sweatpants, exposing his massive, thick rod that stood at attention. Constance was uncertain if she could take it all in. Ahyende removed her dress as she lay across the bed, displaying her full bare breasts and black lace thong. He slid her panties off and tossed them on the floor. He took time to admire her body, running his hands across every inch of it before he took a nosedive between her legs. Constance clasped the sheets with one hand and his locs with the other. Ahyende's tongue felt like magic.

He stopped briefly and whispered in her ear, "Don't be afraid to cum while I'm down there. I want to taste you." He traced his tongue back down her body before returning to her pleasure point.

Constance tried to refrain from climaxing as

Ahyende's tongue entered her velvet walls, but the sensation was far too great for her, and she erupted like a volcano.

He moaned with pleasure as the warm, sweet goodness ran down his chin.

Ahyende rose from her thighs, mouth glistening. He cautiously inched his massive rod between Constance's walls, relishing in the warmth. He moved his body slowly as he slid back and forth in her wetness.

Constance ran her nails across his back as she achieved ecstasy. "Harder," she moaned.

Ahyende did as he was told, and she was able to take in more of his massiveness. "Harder," she moaned louder.

Once again, he followed orders.

Constance opened her legs wider as Ahyende thrust stronger. Their hearts pounded as their senses were intoxicated by the smell of sweat and sex in the air. Ahyende began to thrust even harder until all his love was enveloped in Constance's warm, wet walls. He moved his body to a slow and steady beat that only their hearts could hear. Each pump increased the mounds of pleasure growing inside her. Ahyende placed Constance's legs on his shoulders and picked her up with one quick swoop. His thrusts were mighty as she bounced on his rod, his hands cupping her buttocks for support. Her moans increased into wails of pleasure, and with one last powerful thrust, Ahyende released his goodness into the walls of his pristine beauty.

Sexually exhausted, they held each other and fell

asleep. In the morning, they enjoyed each other again before Ahyende got out of bed to make breakfast.

Constance arrived at the kitchen table wearing one of Ahyende's t-shirts.

"So, how are you feeling?" he asked.

"Happy," Constance replied. "And, honestly, it is something I haven't felt in a long time." Constance leaned in and gave Ahyende a deep kiss. "I love you," she said.

"I love you, too," he replied.

Never before had Constance been filled with such happiness. She couldn't wait to meet with Marvin and break off their engagement. Ahyende filled the void she'd had for years, and Constance wanted to share her life with him.

As she left for work that morning, she called Marvin and left him a message asking him to meet her for dinner. Today was going to be the day that changed her life forever.

CHAPTER NINE

Smoke and Mirrors

Constance arrived at work feeling optimistic about the decision she had made; however, there was only one problem: Marvin had yet to call her back. Constance called his cell again and received the voicemail.

That's odd, she thought. Maybe he was in a meeting, so she called his office.

Marvin's assistant answered. "Blackburn and Associates."

"Hey, Cheryl. It's Constance. May I speak to Marvin, please?"

"I'm sorry, but Mr. Wallace is out of the office today."

"Is he in a meeting?"

"No, ma'am. He didn't come in today. As a matter of fact, he called this morning to inform me he would be taking a personal day and not to forward any personal calls."

Constance was puzzled. "Well, do you know when he'll be back in the office?"

"No, but I assume it won't be long. After all, he can't take too much time away from work now that he's a partner."

Partner? Constance was shocked. She knew that she and Marvin hadn't spoken much in the past weeks, but why wouldn't he tell her he'd made partner?

"You must be so proud of him," said Cheryl.

"Huh?" Constance was still stunned. "I'm sorry. I mean of course. This is everything he's worked so hard for." Constance dared not let Cheryl know she had no idea of Marvin's promotion. "I'm sure you're excited, too. This means a big promotion for you."

"And not to mention a bigger office." Cheryl laughed.

They ended their conversation with Constance feeling more confused than ever. She thought of calling Mrs. Wallace to see what information she could get from her but quickly decided against it. Instead, she sent Marvin a text message: Call me back when you get this, Partner.

Within minutes, her cell phone rang.

"Hey, baby. How are you?" Marvin asked.

"Honestly, I'm a little confused," Constance replied. "I'm racking my brain as to why my fiancé didn't tell me he made partner."

"Well, I was going to surprise you with the news, but it seems Cheryl ruined that."

"How do you know it was Cheryl?" Constance asked.

"Because, other than my mother, she is the only

person who knows, and I can bet money you didn't talk to Mother. Speaking of which, you need to call her. She really wants to have lunch with you soon."

"She has my number. Why hasn't she called me?"

"Mother thinks you don't like her and, with all due respect, Connie, you could make more of an effort to develop a relationship with her. After all, we will all be family soon."

"That reminds me," Constance interrupted. "Did you get my message about dinner?"

"Yes, sweetheart, I did, but, unfortunately, I won't be able to make it. I took a trip of leisure with one of the senior partners. We flew out to Miami for a few days."

"You're in Florida, and you didn't tell me?"

"Must we do this now, dear? It was last minute, and it's something all the senior partners do for the new partners. It's a Blackburn tradition. I promise I'll call you as soon as I return."

"And when will that be?" Constance asked. Just then, she heard a woman giggle on Marvin's end of the line. "Who the hell is that!" she screeched.

"It's just some girls walking by. Don't get ghetto. It isn't very becoming," Marvin scolded. "Look, I have to go. I'll call you when I land, promise."

Marvin hung up, and their conversation ended leaving Constance perplexed. She was fuming and wanted to go into a rage, but she remembered the decision she had made to be with Ahyende and her mood softened. Her break up with Marvin would have to wait. She decided to call Ahyende and inform him of her situation with Marvin, but Alicia interrupted her.

"Hey, Constance. There's someone here to see you."

Constance sighed. "Does it have to be me? I'm in the middle of something."

"Well, she said she wanted to speak with the owner," Alicia replied. "If you like, I can tell her you're busy ..."

"No, don't do that. Tell her I'm on my way." To herself, she muttered, "What now?" She had no clue of what the customer wanted. She just hoped it wasn't a complaint.

She was met by a petite blonde whose face she remembered but she couldn't recall from where.

"Hi, Constance!" The woman was far too chipper to be a disgruntled customer. "You may not remember me. My name is Loren Prescott. We met outside the coffeehouse. I gave you my parking spot."

"Yes, I remember," Constance replied, dropping her guard. "I hope you've come in to take advantage of that discount."

"My credit card just got a work out." She laughed. "I just wanted you to know that I am absolutely enamored with your boutique."

Constance was pleased with the compliment. "Why, thank you. Please, don't be a stranger."

"Oh, I'll be back. You can bet on it," Loren replied. "As a matter of fact, I wanted to ask if you've ever rented out your space for special events."

"I haven't had anything 'special' here in a while."

"I only ask because I have a client who is an artist;

however, none of the galleries here will give him a chance to display his work. I feel your boutique will be the perfect background to display his art amongst the many beautiful items here. Not only will it give him notoriety, but it will also be great advertising for your business."

"I like the way you think, Loren. I'd have to see this art before I can make a decision, though."

"No problem. He has a small studio in the Heights. We can meet there this Saturday if you aren't busy." Loren reached into her purse for a business card and quickly scribbled an address on the back. "Here's the address, and my number is on the front of the card. Call me when you decide on a time."

"I'm actually free any time this Saturday. Will two o'clock work for you?" Constance asked.

"Two is perfect! I'll see you then."

The two women shook hands, and Loren went on her way.

Constance was excited. This was just the kind of publicity she needed to bring more business to her store. She felt good about her encounter with Loren and looked forward to their meeting. Loren's visit seemed to be the thing Constance needed to turn her day around. For a moment, she had almost forgotten to call Ahyende and fill him in on her dilemma with Marvin.

Constance and Ahyende decided to meet for lunch. She felt this conversation was too important to discuss over the phone. The café was jam packed with the lunch crowd, making it nearly impossible to get a table.

Fortunately, Constance was able to grab a table up front. Usually, she and Ahyende grabbed a booth in the far back for privacy, but today, she didn't care if anyone saw them together. She and Ahyende were in love, and she was ready to let the world know.

It wasn't long before Ahyende arrived at the café. Constance noticed him the moment he stepped through the door. His clothes looked impeccable clinging to his statuesque frame. His mere presence astounded her.

Constance stood and waved. Ahyende couldn't contain his smile as he laid eyes on her. The couple greeted each other with a passionate kiss.

"Damn, that felt good," he said.

"Yes, it did," Constance agreed.

"What's all this? No corner booth, kisses in public ... Could it be official that you're all mine?"

"That's what we need to talk about."

Ahyende's face was shadowed by apprehension.

"I called Marvin to tell him, but he didn't give me the chance."

Ahyende seemed annoyed. "What do you mean he didn't give you the chance?"

"What I mean is he blew me off, as usual. It seems he's in Florida, and he isn't there alone."

"And what does that have to do with us?"

"Absolutely nothing. I tried to tell him, but there was a woman giggling in the background, and when I asked him about it, he told me it was nothing and quickly got off the phone."

Ahyende was beginning to lose his patience. "So, why didn't you just quickly tell him it was over between the two of you? And why are you so concerned about this so-called woman in the background?"

Ahyende's reaction caught her by surprise. "Wait … what? Ahyende, I told you I love you. I don't care if Marvin has a hundred other women; it's over between us."

"Is that why you're still wearing his ring?"

Ahyende's behavior puzzled her. "I was only wearing this ring for appearances. It means absolutely nothing to me." She reached across the table and held Ahyende's hand. "You are the man I want to spend my life with. You and only you. This ring is a symbol of ownership, not love."

She removed her engagement ring and placed it inside her purse. "I will tell Marvin about us as soon as he gets back. You have my word on that. It's just me and you." She leaned across the table and gave Ahyende another kiss. "I tell you what, why don't I come over tonight, and we can spend the entire evening together."

"I like the sound of that," Ahyende replied, beaming.

The two enjoyed their lunch and parted ways. Constance left the restaurant feeling confident and more convinced than ever that she was making the right decision.

That evening, she arrived at Ahyende's place, and he greeted her with a smile and kiss. The loft was impeccable, eclectic in design, yet every piece of furniture complemented the next. The view was breathtaking, boasting the Houston skyline from every corner of the room. As Constance moved further into the space, she could hear jazz playing on the speakers.

"What smells so good?" she asked, making her way to the kitchen.

"I'm making dinner for you. Nothing special, just grilled chicken breast served on a bed of sautéed baby spinach and kale and homemade strawberry sorbet for dessert. I hope you will enjoy.

"Oh, I'm sure I will," she replied.

They sat down to dinner at one of Ahyende's hand-crafted tables. Constance was in awe of the craftsmanship. The base of the dining table was shaped like an arc supporting the glass top. It was unlike anything she had ever seen. "Did you make this?" she asked.

"Yes, I did," he replied proudly. "Do you like it?"

"I love it. It's sleek and modern yet unique. What is it made of?"

"It's a curly eastern maple finish with aniline dyes and a pre-catalyzed lacquer."

Constance had no idea what he was talking about, but it turned her on to hear him speak that way.

The two indulged in conversation over dinner and Boudreaux Blanc. After dinner, Ahyende treated her to a much-needed foot rub. She lay back and enjoyed every minute of her pampering. Constance couldn't believe how fortunate she was to have met a man like him.

"I have one more thing to make our evening complete," he told her. "You sit tight, and I'll be right back.

Within minutes, Ahyende returned downstairs with a bandana in hand.

"I need you to put this on," he instructed.

Constance did as she was told and secured the bandana over her eyes.

"Now, take my hand and follow me."

Ahyende carefully led her up the stairs. He removed the blindfold. She was surprised to learn that she had been led into the bathroom. Lilac and lavender scented candles were lit on the vanity and around a garden tub filled with bubbles. Ahyende didn't speak any words as he slowly undressed her. He kissed her feverishly while meticulously removing her clothing and her lace bra and panties. Constance placed her hand on his rod and began to massage his engorged massiveness.

He gently moved her hand aside and whispered in her ear, "Tonight isn't about me. Tonight is all about you."

He led Constance to the bathtub, and she slid inside. She welcomed the tingling sensation of the scorching hot water against her skin and let out a deep sigh. Ahyende knelt next to her and began to massage her temples, making his way down to her shoulders. Her body seemed frail compared to his. She was, to him, as delicate as a flower, and he took special care to be gentle with her.

Ahyende grabbed a bath sponge and caressed her back, working his way around to her breasts, her stomach, her thighs, and all the places in between. Constance's mind was in a whirlwind. No man had ever taken the time to lavish so much attention on her. She kept her eyes closed as he bathed her for fear that if she opened them, she may wake up and find that this was all just a dream. After her bath, he dried her body with a lush towel and dressed her in a black silk robe. Ahyende placed succulent kisses on Constance's lips and led her into his bedroom.

"You have to lie down for this part," he told her.

She inched her way across the king-sized bed and lay down eagerly, anticipating what was next. He disrobed his flower and instructed her to lie on her stomach. Constance obliged, and her body was greeted by warm silken oil. Ahyende massaged her arms, shoulders, back, buttocks, legs, and thighs.

Her body ached for him to enter her. She could no longer stand the intensity. She had to feel him inside her. She rolled over and grabbed him around the neck, pulling him close to her. "I need to feel you," she whispered.

"Uh uh, not tonight," he whispered back. "I told you, tonight is all about you."

He positioned Constance back onto her stomach and continued to massage every inch of her body. Ahyende's masculine hands found every pressure point, and with every caress, the stresses of the day melted away. Once he could tell her body was completely relaxed, he placed his arms under her thighs and pulled her body closer to him. He plunged his face between Constance's thighs, separating her feminine lips with his tongue. She came instantaneously. She could feel her juices trickling down her thighs. Ahyende let out a deep moan as her moistness saturated his lips. Her orgasm enhanced his sexual desire, and he put more pressure on her clit, being careful to lick every wet drop that ran between her legs.

He could no longer resist the tantalizing beauty that lay before him. His massive erection throbbed, longing to feel the moist treasure that hid between her thighs. Quickly, Ahyende pulled down his sweatpants and entered her from behind. She gasped at the unexpected sensation, and he moaned as her moist walls engulfed his stiffness. Ahyende tried to contain his excitement, but her warmth was too overwhelming, and he found himself ready to climax.

Remembering that hadn't bothered to wear protection, he removed himself and released his stickiness upon the backside of his love. The two lovers collapsed and fell asleep in each other's arms.

The alluring smell of bacon roused Constance from her sex-induced coma. She slid on the robe from the night before and went downstairs. Ahyende stood in the kitchen wearing pajama pants and slippers, awaiting her arrival. He had prepared a breakfast of bacon, eggs, bagels, and fresh fruit.

"This looks delicious," she said.

"A breakfast fit for a queen," he replied.

"Does that make you my king?"

"If you're willing to have me."

Constance smiled and gave Ahyende a passionate kiss. "Does that answer your question?" she asked with a grin.

"I'm not quite sure. I've always been a slow learner," he joked. "Maybe you should kiss me again."

They laughed and sat to enjoy breakfast. Constance was famished from last night's excursion, but Ahyende hardly ate at all. He kept looking at Constance, smiling. Not accustomed to this sort of undivided attention, she blushed and looked down at her plate.

"Am I making you uncomfortable, Miss McGuire?" he asked.

"A little."

"Why is that?"

"I'm just—I'm just not used to a man looking at me the way you do. I notice men looking at me all the time, and most of them have a look of lust in their eyes when they see me. But you, when you look at me, it's more like you're looking *into* me, if that makes any sense."

"It makes perfect sense. Constance, when I look at you, I see more than your beauty and your body. I see a woman who is kind, caring, and ambitious. I look at you, and I see you as my wife and the mother of my children. I look at you and see the person I'm going to spend the rest of my life with."

"You have no idea how that makes me feel to hear you say that," she said between gasps for air.

"One day, I'm going to do more than just say it. I'm going to prove it to you. I'm going to go to your father and ask his permission for your hand, and then I'm going to propose to you. Then after we're married, I'm going to put a baby inside you. But before any of this can happen, you have to give back that ring to Marvin."

Constance got up from her seat and sat on Ahyende's lap. "I told you, as soon as he gets back, it's as good as done. I promise."

Ahyende gave Constance a hug and held her close. "I love you," he whispered softly in her ear.

"And I love you, too. Now, what should we do today?" she chirped. "I'm tired of meeting in secret places. I want us to go out and enjoy the day together. I'm in love, and I want the whole world to know!"

"Are you sure? I mean that's a big step and, technically, you're still engaged."

"I've never been more sure of anything in my life."

"Okay, let me get dressed, and we can go over to your place and decide where to spend the day from there."

Ahyende raced upstairs. As soon as he was out of her sight, Constance went to her purse and pulled out her cell phone to call Marvin. His phone went straight to voicemail.

"We need to talk when you get back," was all she said and hung up. It wasn't long before Ahyende was downstairs, dressed in jeans, a fresh button-down shirt, and a pair of casual shoes.

They left his apartment hand in hand as they made their way to the parking garage. Constance felt elated by the warmth of Ahyende's palm against hers. She'd never felt such joy over something so small, and she wondered if Ahyende was feeling the same way. At that moment, he gave her hand a kiss. This was the type of connection Constance had longed for. She didn't have to wonder how Ahyende felt about her or if his affection was genuine because he took every opportunity to let her know where he stood. She began to fantasize about a future with the man she loved, where they would have their wedding, how their children would look. The two of them would live a lifetime of love and happiness. Finally, she would have the ideal life she'd always dreamed of, a life unlike her parents'. She would be married to a man who was loyal and cared more about her than his own pleasures.

As Constance approached her car, she caught sight of someone familiar, and it stopped her cold. Before her stood two men exchanging a deep, passionate kiss. She couldn't completely make out one of the men because his back was to her, but she could clearly see the other. She blinked several times to be sure that what she was seeing was, in fact, real. Constance couldn't believe it. One of the men locked in the passionate embrace was Yvette's husband, Steve.

She quickly hid next to the nearest car and motioned for Ahyende to do the same. She took out her cell and immediately began snapping pictures.

"Connie, what is going on? Why are we hiding, and why are you taking pictures of complete strangers?" he asked.

"Did you see those two men kissing?"

"Yes."

"That's no stranger. One of them is my best friend's husband."

"Oh. Now, I can understand why we're hiding."

Constance could hear a car drive away, and she made a mad dash to her car, making sure to get a good look at the other man. Sadly, his was a face she had never seen before.

"Do you know that guy?" she asked Ahyende?

"I've seen him around the building, but I don't know him personally."

Constance gave her car keys to Ahyende. "Can you drive, please? I need time to process all this."

"Are you going to tell your friend?"

"Yes, of course! I have to, don't I?"

Ahyende opened the car door for Constance, and she groaned as she plopped her body onto the passenger seat. "They just had a baby," she said.

Ahyende leaned over and gave her a kiss on the cheek. "You'll figure out what to do. Take some time to pray and think it through. You know we can spend the day together some other time."

"Are you crazy? I'm not going to let this interfere with our time. I've waited months for this. I'm not going to let anything come between us, ever."

"You promise?"

"You have my word," Constance replied as they drove away.

CHAPTER TEN

All Good Things
Come to an End

Once home, Constance quickly showered and changed into her favorite maxi dress and a pair of chic sandals. She dusted a light powder onto her face, applied clear mascara to her luscious lashes, and added a little rosebud salve to her lips. She dabbed a little bit on her cheeks for good measure and was about to head downstairs when the image of Steve's make-out session replayed in her brain.

Constance quickly knelt at her vanity and began to pray. "Father God in heaven, I don't want to keep Yvette in the dark about what I have seen. I ask, Dear God, that Steve delivers this emotional blow to his wife so I won't have to. However, if it is me that You choose to tell her, I pray that You grant me the strength, courage, and wisdom to do so. In Jesus's name, I pray. Amen."

Ahyende waited patiently for Constance, thumbing through the numerous *Vogue* and *Oprah* magazines on the coffee table. He was halfway through an article about improving your skin's elasticity when she met him downstairs. Ever the gentleman, he stood as she entered the room.

"You look amazing," he said and planted a kiss on her cheek. "So, what do you want to do today?"

"I think I should be your personal tour guide. I'm going to show you everything that I love about this city. We can't get it all done in a day, so I figure we can start with the Museum District and see where we end up from there."

"I'm game."

"Okay then," she squealed. "Let me grab my keys, and away we'll go."

Constance and Ahyende left her place arm in arm. The situation with Steve still didn't sit well with her but, for now, she let it go. She had prayed on it, moved on, and was waiting for God to tell her what her next move (if any) should be.

"Wait," she said as she re-entered her key into the deadbolt. "I forgot something."

Constance ran upstairs to her bedroom, removed the five-carat Tiffany solitaire from her purse and placed it back into its little blue box. She put the box in her nightstand drawer. It felt as if a ton of bricks had been lifted from her shoulders. She quickly made her way back downstairs to Ahyende. "Now, I'm ready," she told him, and they hurried off on their excursion.

A trip to the Museum of Fine Arts was just what Ahyende needed for artistic inspiration. The precision of the Greek and Roman statues and the vibrancy of the Byzantine Frescoes sparked a multitude of ideas and emotions for his next furniture collection.

Constance was also feeling energized. The African and Native American art moved her and evoked a sense of pride, while the regality of the European exhibit filled her with excitement. She was mesmerized by the Arts of Europe collection. The human-like quality of William Bouguereau's The Elder Sister gave her chills.

"I've always loved this one," she said to Ahyende as they stood in front of the painting.

"Why?" he asked.

"The detail is impeccable. It's as if Bouguereau trapped his daughter's soul in the canvas. I always feel like she is looking right at me, beckoning me with her eyes. The clarity is unreal. I've seen photographs and 3D TVs that aren't that sharp."

"Wow, you've really studied this piece."

"I remember the first time I saw it. I was six. My parents had just gotten into a huge fight. It seemed my father had made a jewelry purchase that my mother hadn't received. Anyway, my mom packed a suitcase with some of our things and told my father she'd had enough. We got into the car and drove down Fifty-Nine. She told me we were going to visit my grandparents who lived in Victoria. Instead of going to my grandparents', we ended up here at the museum. We walked around, and I was in complete awe of everything because it was my first time being here. My mother studied art and archaeology in college, so she was able to give me insight into the art and artifacts. She'd had ambitions of owning an art gallery, but my father was against it. He said that as a pastor's wife, her job was to be First Lady. So she gave in to my father's wishes and gave up on her dreams because it was what a 'Christian wife' was expected to do.

"Somehow, during my mother's unofficial tour, I got lost. I was so afraid, I started to panic. I went from room to room, searching for my mama, and in one room, I turned around and the girl in this portrait was staring me in the face. I saw her and could not move. It was as if her stare had me locked into a trance. I was standing right here in front of this very painting when my mother found me. I braced myself for a whooping, but she was more relieved than upset. After that, we left the museum and went back home.

"I didn't have all the details, but I knew Daddy had broken her heart, and instead of leaving, she stayed. She went back to him, only to be subjected to the same treatment time and time again. One day, I overheard them arguing, and I remember her saying, 'Gerry, you do what you want, but I'll be damned if you ever bring a baby home! You better take care of this because I'm not helping you raise another woman's child!' Isn't that crazy? Daddy could do all the dirt in the world with any woman he saw fit, as long as no one saw. But to have an outside child would be proof of his infidelities, and Mama would not dare be made to be a public embarrassment."

Ahyende held Constance close and kissed her on the forehead. "It's crazy how the sins of our fathers affect us."

Constance let out a deep breath. "Let's go get lunch. What are you in the mood for?"

"Well, this is *your* city. What do you like to eat around here?"

"I know just the place." She smiled.

Within minutes, they arrived at Constance's favorite Vietnamese restaurant, which caught Ahyende off guard. "Interesting. Would you believe me if I told you I've never had Vietnamese food?"

"You've got to be kidding me. A man who prepares gourmet cuisine and is an aficionado of exotic woods has never eaten Vietnamese food?"

He chuckled. "Nope, never. It's not that I don't want to. It's on my to-do list. I've just never found the time."

"Well, you're in for a treat because this happens to be the best Vietnamese restaurant in the city."

They walked into the restaurant, and a friendly hostess greeted them. She escorted them to the nearest booth and gave them their menus.

Ahyende wasted no time opening his. "So, what's good here?" he asked Constance. "Better yet, why don't you surprise me?"

"I can assure you that you will not be disappointed

with my selection. The appetizer portions are so large there will be no need for an entrée."

"I seriously doubt that. I'm famished. You can't be this big and fine and not have an appetite," he joked.

"We'll see if you can hang."

The waiter came over to take their order. Constance ordered *goi ga* (chilled cabbage chicken salad) and *banh xeo* (a Vietnamese crepe with stuffed prawn, shrimp, bean sprouts, and onions) in perfect Vietnamese.

The server was quite impressed. "Very good," he said, referring more to her pronunciations than her menu selections.

Ahyende was impressed as well. "You speak Vietnamese?" he asked as the waiter walked away.

Constance laughed. "Oh, not at all. I just eat a lot of ethnic foods, and I like to order them properly. I also learned, very early, that other cultures appreciate it when you take the time to learn their language."

Her theory must have been true because their food arrived quickly and was piping hot. It was all more than Ahyende was expecting. Constance hadn't lied about the portions; they were huge, and the presentation was eye catching. He enjoyed the crepes and dove into the salad but was full after the third bite.

Constance sat with her head in her hand as she observed Ahyende slightly push his plate away.

"What's the matter, Big Fine?" she asked. "Are you full?"

"Nah, I'm just letting my food digest."

"Well, while you're letting your food digest, I'll get a to-go container and one for you, too, just in case you change your mind."

Ahyende agreed with a defeated nod.

"So, how did you like the museum?" she asked as they waited for the server.

"It was more than I was expecting. We were in there like, what, three hours, and it felt like half that time."

"I know. I love it there. You can just get lost in yourself."

"Exactly! Right now, my mind is going one hundred miles an hour. I have to go create while it's fresh on my brain."

Constance's face dropped. "Well, I was hoping we could spend the entire day together, but I won't intrude on your work."

"Baby, don't be like that. I want to make something for you, not for profit. Something personal, so when you look at it, you'll always remember this day and this moment. What we ate, what the weather was like, our conversations. It will be better than any picture or painting in any museum. I'll work for a few hours this afternoon, and tonight, we can make hot, passionate, mind-blowing love to each other." Ahyende was not a man who struggled with words.

Constance motioned for the waiter. "Check, please!"

His studio wasn't far from his loft. They entered a freight elevator and rode up three shaky floors before it stopped. He raised the gate on the elevator. "After you," he said, motioning for Constance to exit.

She carefully stepped off the freight elevator and directly into the dimly lit workspace. The smell of cedar, maple, and other woods invaded her nostrils. Constance sneezed from the dust in the air.

"Bless you."

"Thank you," she replied, surveying the room with the amazement of a wide-eyed child.

"So, what do you think?" Ahyende asked, full of pride.

"It is remarkable. To think, you do all this by hand. There is no mass production, no assembly lines, or heavy machinery. It's amazing."

"If you like, you can stay and watch me work."

"No, I couldn't. I want to be surprised when you're done."

"That's cool." He nodded. "Let me just show you what I have in mind."

Ahyende walked around a brick wall at the rear of the room. He wasn't gone long before he came back with a large tree stump. "This is microberlinia brazzavillensis, also known as zebrawood. It's found in West Africa and can grow up to one hundred fifty feet tall. Take a good look at it now, because you won't recognize it when I'm done."

Constance ran her hand across the tree trunk's rough exterior. "What do you think you'll make?" she asked.

"Uh uh. You want to be surprised, remember?"

"Well, I can't wait." She gave Ahyende a kiss. "Would you like me to pick you up later and give you a ride to your place?"

"Nah, it's cool. It's only a few blocks. I can walk. I'll call you when I'm done."

They kissed once more, and Constance rode the three rickety floors back down the freight elevator and got into her car. As she turned the key, she noticed Ahyende watching her from his window. She blew him a kiss, and he pretended to catch it with his hand and place it over his heart.

Before driving away, she said a quick prayer. "Dear God, thank you for this kind, sensitive, God-fearing man."

While driving, she called Yvette and prayed she could play it cool around her. She took a few deep breaths for reassurance. "Hey, girl. How's my godbaby?"

"She's nursing now. I'm doing well, too. Thanks for asking," Yvette sassed.

"Now, you know I meant you, too. I was out and wanted to stop by."

"Okay, we'll be here."

That wasn't so bad. I just hope I'm able to keep it together when I see her.

Constance made a quick stop at Janie and Jack to pick up a few things for baby Marie. After that, she made a stop at Essentials to purchase a bauble necklace and a few candles, soaps, and incense she knew Yvette liked.

"I'm only passing through," she assured Alicia. "This is not an attempt to check up on you."

"I'm not worried," Alicia replied jokingly. "As you can see, I have everything under control. Before I forget, a lady by the name of Loren Prescott called to confirm your meeting tomorrow."

"Did anyone else call?" she asked, hoping Marvin had called the shop.

"Nope. Just business as usual."

Constance couldn't understand what could be keeping him from calling her. Since they'd spoken last, she hadn't heard from him at all. He hadn't even sent a text message. Fortunately, he would be back tomorrow, and she could see him after her meeting with Loren.

"Keep up the good work," she teased and left the store.

Yvette came to the door with Marie bundled snuggly in an organic all-white Baby K'tan.

"I've come bearing gifts." Constance revealed the large shopping bag she had concealed behind her back.

"You're going to have this little girl spoiled rotten," Yvette said with a smile.

"Oh, and there's something in here for you, too," Constance added.

Yvette began to cry. "Hormones," she said. "I'm crying more now than I ever did when I was pregnant."

Constance reached into her purse and gave Yvette a Kleenex.

"Thank you," she said between sniffles and sobs.

There was an uneasiness in the room, and Constance was unsure of what to say to ease the tension. She wanted to tell Yvette about Steve but wasn't sure how. "Would you like me to lay the baby down?" she asked, noticing that Marie was sound asleep.

"Sure," replied Yvette, seeming more relaxed.

Constance took the baby to her lavishly decorated nursery and laid her in her crib, careful not to rouse her from her sleep. She returned to the living room where Yvette sat with her feet resting on an ottoman.

"So how's work?" Yvette asked.

Things are going so well that I'm actually looking to open a second location. I've met with the realtor, and now we're playing a game of numbers with the developers."

Yvette smiled. "I'm so proud of you. All those late nights we would stay up in our dorm room planning our futures. You always said you would be a successful entrepreneur, and I would marry the man of my dreams and have a large family. It looks like we're both well on our way to our dreams," she said, beginning to cry again.

This time, Constance knew it wasn't the hormones. "Yvette, what's wrong?" she asked, dreading the response.

"I have everything I ever wanted, and I am completely miserable," she confessed.

Constance became overridden with guilt. She sat closer to her friend. "Yvette, you have a beautiful, healthy baby girl. You have a stunning home and a husband who lavishes you with the best of everything. Hell, I often wish I had what you have."

Yvette laughed. "You want what I have," she said, mimicking Constance. "Well, if Marvin is anything like Steve, I'm sure you'll get it."

"What do you mean?" Constance hoped this was leeway to inform Yvette of what she knew.

"Steve is having an affair."

"An affair? How can you be sure?"

Yvette jumped up from the sofa and began pacing the floor. "Oh, I'm sure. His routine and behaviors have completely changed. He's always up at two and three o'clock in the morning on his laptop, 'searching for sales leads.' Whenever he's on his phone, he leaves the room. And when he isn't on the phone, he's constantly sending and receiving text messages! I'm no fool, Connie. I just wish I knew who she was. Maybe I could talk to her, get her to leave him alone, and then he'd have to stay committed to me, to our family."

Constance saw this as the answer to her prayer. "Sit down, Yvette. I want to show you something."

Yvette sat, and Constance uploaded the pictures from her cell phone. She showed them to Yvette and watched as she massaged her temples in disbelief.

"Constance, what is this?"

She didn't know how to explain what was clearly before her friend's own eyes. Slowly, she looked at Yvette. "Honey, it's Steve ... with another man."

Yvette's face grew white, and her palms began to sweat. "Is this some sick joke?"

"I wish it was, but I witnessed it myself," Constance replied solemnly.

Anger began to rise in Yvette. "And how long have you known this?"

"I saw it this morning as I was—" she stopped abruptly. Constance still hadn't told a soul about her involvement with Ahyende. She wanted to break the news to Marvin first. "Does it matter? Now you know what you have been feeling is true."

Disgust blanketed Yvette's face. "And you were able to go about your day as if nothing happened while I sat here with a newborn, crying my eyes out because my husband didn't come home last night? Tell me, Connie, what was more important to you than sharing this with me the minute you found out?"

Yvette was enraged. It was a side of her Constance had never seen before. She had to tell her the truth. Besides, once she broke things off with Marvin, everyone would know anyway.

"I saw Steve as I was leaving with Ahyende. The guy in the picture lives in his building."

"You didn't tell me about my husband because you've been busy hanging out with your secret boyfriend? And here I was thinking Marvin wasn't good enough for you. I would never do anything like this to you." Tears rolled down Yvette's face. "Get out of my house!"

Constance was in a state of shock. This was not the way she thought it would be. She wanted to tell Yvette how confused she was about the situation and she didn't know what to do. She thought if she explained to her that she needed time to gather her thoughts and give Steve the opportunity to come clean that everything would be okay. She wanted to say all these things, but she couldn't find the words.

"Get out!" Yvette screamed. Her voice carried into

the nursery, waking Marie. Her shrill cry came through on the baby monitor. "My daughter and I do *not* need you in our lives," she said, thrusting the shopping bag into Constance's chest.

"I'm sorry," Constance whispered as she grabbed her purse and headed for the door.

Yvette followed closely. "Don't worry about returning my key. The locks will be changed immediately," she said and slammed the door.

Constance was in disbelief. What had she done to deserve to be treated in such a way? She got into her car and called Ahyende. He didn't pick up. She thought about going back over to the studio but remembered he said he would walk back to his place. She tried reaching Tameka, but her phone went directly to voicemail. Constance hung up, deciding not to leave a message. No one was available. This was something she had to figure out on her own.

That night, she didn't bother to pray. As she lay in bed, eyes heavy yet unable to sleep, she thought about how to make things right with Yvette but couldn't come to a solution. Finally, she called her mother and filled her in. She told her every detail of that day, including spending time with Ahyende.

Mrs. McGuire sat silently on the opposite end of the phone. She didn't utter a single word until Constance was done.

"Baby, I love you, and I know Yvette is one of your dearest friends, and you had nothing but the best intentions; however, you were wrong."

Constance was stunned by her mother's words. "Wrong? Mama, how was I wrong? I saw my best friend's husband do a detestable thing. I prayed on it, and when the opportunity posed itself, I saw it as God answering my prayer, and I exposed him for the lying piece of crap he is."

Mildred McGuire chuckled. "So, you're saying that Steve is 'detestable' and a 'lying piece of crap,' but you're the one who saw him in an adulterous act while you were out cheating on your fiancé? Well ain't that the pot calling the kettle black?"

"What? Mama, my situation is completely different. Marvin is a world-class jerk, and I called to break things off with him, but he hung up on me."

"Connie, you know that I'm the last one to judge, but if you were going to break up with Marvin, you would have done so already. I understand that you're trying to be a lady about it and spare his feelings, but the truth of the matter is no matter how you do it, he's going to be hurt. You could've written him an honest, heartfelt letter and left it under his door."

"Mama, that is so crass. We've been together too long. He deserves more than that."

"When a person wants something bad enough, they find a way. You are keeping Marvin in your back pocket in case things don't turn out well with you and this other man. You honestly believe that God appointed you to call Steve out on his mess when you are doing the exact same thing? Baby, God doesn't work like that. What you did was self-righteous. Maybe witnessing his infidelity is God's way of putting a mirror up to your face and having you come clean. John eight-seven: 'Let any one of you who is without sin be the first to throw a stone.'"

Constance fell silent. She knew her mother was right.

Mildred continued. "When you went home and prayed, what you should have done was thank God for showing you your own deceptive ways through some-one else, and you should've repented and left this other man alone completely until you got things squared away with Marvin. Baby, what you're doing has disrupted the lives of many people and may have cost you a genuine friendship. If this man you're seeing really is sent from God, would loving him cost you so much turmoil and confusion?"

Constance began to speak.

"Don't answer now. I want you to meditate on that." Mildred let out a sigh. "You know, sometimes I think I've failed you as a mother. If I would have left your father years ago instead of putting up with all his infidelities, you could've had a chance to see what true love is. No relationship is perfect, but love does not hurt. And if a man can't love you with the same kindness and gentleness as the Heavenly Father, then he doesn't deserve you. You think about what I said. Goodnight. I love you."

Constance had an uneasy feeling in the pit of her stomach. Her throat was parched and her lips dry. Before she hung up, she said, "I love you, too, Mama" in a raspy breath. She had a decision to make, yet she was still unsure of what her decision would be.

CHAPTER ELEVEN

What's Done in the Dark . . .

The next morning, Constance couldn't shake her mother's words. What if Ahyende wasn't heaven sent. Yes, theirs was a complicated love, but no relationship was perfect. Constance's parents had been married for thirty-five years, and they'd had their ups and downs, but they were still together.

"I have to make this decision for myself based on my own beliefs," she thought aloud. "And I know what I have to do."

Constance quickly showered, dressed, and made her way toward the door. Her cell phone rang before she could insert her key into the lock. It was Marvin.

"Back so soon?" she asked.

"I missed you."

"Really? Is that why I haven't heard from you?"

"Constance, please, let's not do this. I had to let the

partners see that I was my own man. Do you know how emasculating it would be to have the partners see me phoning my fiancée every hour? We're one step closer to our dream of public office. I can't let that slip away."

"*We* ... I wasn't aware that it was also my dream to sit on the Senate."

"No, your dream is to be the wife of a very influential man and bear his children." Marvin chuckled. "And with one erratic move, that path can be altered."

Constance was tight lipped on the other end of the phone.

"Lighten up, Connie. It was a joke ... laced with a bit of truth."

"You know, I never found your humor amusing, Marvin."

"Tell you what, why don't you meet me for lunch at two?"

"I can't. I have a meeting today. Can we make it dinner instead? Is seven okay?"

Marvin was beginning to sound exasperated. "You're inconveniencing me. I had plans, but I think I can move them around. I hope you know that you owe me, so wear something sexy."

"Whatever, Marvin. I'll see you tonight," Constance said as she began to hang up.

"One thing before you go."

She had grown annoyed with their conversation. "What's that?"

"Why haven't you talked to Mother? She told me she's

called you all weekend, and you haven't returned any of her phone calls."

Constance was confused. "So you've spoken with your mother, but you couldn't call me or accept any of my calls?"

"It's nothing like that. I called my mother as I was leaving the hotel. I had to. You know how much she worries about me."

Constance shook her head and sighed. "I'll call her tomorrow. See you at dinner. You pick the spot."

"No problem. And don't forget what I said. Wear something sexy."

Constance didn't reply to his remark. She simply hung up, got into her car, and drove to work.

She was the first to arrive at the boutique. She immediately made her way to her office to disarm the alarm and remove the tills from the safe. After counting down the registers, she used the landline to call Ahyende. She hadn't heard from him since she'd dropped him off at his studio the day before. His phone went straight to voicemail. Constance was beginning to worry. It was unlike him to not call her, let alone not answer her phone calls. She picked up the phone to call again but didn't want to seem pushy. *Maybe he's just really focused on his project,* she thought. *I'm sure he'll call once he's done.*

Constance went about the responsibilities of opening the store and made her way to the bank to get change. She received a call on her cell while waiting for the teller. She quickly reached into her bag to retrieve her phone, hoping it was Ahyende calling her back. To her dismay, it was an unidentified number.

"Constance McGuire speaking."

"Hi, Constance!" the voice was unfamiliar.

"Yes?"

"It's Loren Prescott. I wanted to touch base with you about our meeting this afternoon."

The meeting ... She'd been so preoccupied with Marvin and Ahyende that she'd forgotten all about the meeting with Loren.

"Hello, Loren." Constance tried not to sound surprised. "Yes, today at two. I received the message you left with my assistant manager."

"Great," Loren replied enthusiastically. "I hope the location isn't too far for you."

Constance hadn't bothered to read the location written on the back of the card Loren gave her. "It's perfect," she lied.

"Fantastic. I told my client about you and your business, and he is eager to meet with you."

"I can't wait. See you this afternoon."

It seemed getting in touch with Ahyende would have to wait. Between her meeting with Loren at two and dinner with Marvin, Constance was unsure how she would find the time to swing by Ahyende's studio. However, she knew she had to find a way because her nerves were becoming more shot with each passing hour.

Business at the boutique was steady, but Constance couldn't focus on her work. She kept replaying her altercation with Yvette and the advice her mother had given her about Ahyende. She went to her office to call Tameka and finally got an answer.

"Hey, girl. What's up?" Tameka asked.

"Well, it's about time. I was beginning to think you'd fallen off the face of the earth. Where have you been?"

"Oh, girl, I was gone for the sorority's membership induction for the weekend. We had a new undergrad line come through, and I decided to go last minute. So what's been going on with you? Have you made any wedding plans?"

Constance sighed. "I don't even know where to begin."

"Well, have you at least picked the colors?"

"No. I've been far too preoccupied with this new store to even begin to plan a wedding."

"Well, a blushing bride should be more enthusiastic about the biggest day of her life."

Constance could sense the sarcasm in Tameka's voice. "MeMe, please. I called you to talk business. I'm meeting with someone today to discuss hosting an event at the shop. I'm going to need someone to take care of the PR. If all is on the up and up, I want you to handle the promotion piece."

"Sure, girl, I can take care of that for you. Just get with me after your meeting so we can discuss things, and I can get a media kit together."

"Sounds good to me. Hey, have you talked to Yvette?"

"Nope, just got back. Haven't had time. Why, what's up?"

"Nothing. Just seeing if you've gone by to see the baby yet."

Tameka was irritated. "Connie, I don't need you checking up on me, telling me how to be a good friend."

Constance released a sigh. "What's been up with you lately? Every time I say something to you, you take it as a personal attack."

"That's because you're always throwing shade at me like you're so much better than me. You out here doing dirt, but all up in the church day after day."

"Look, Tameka, I never said I was better than you, and I'm sorry if you feel that way. Truth be told, I admire your ballsy attitude. I was just ..." Constance was in no mood to continue the conversation. "Look, I'll call you after my meeting."

"You do that," Tameka snapped and hung up.

Lord Jesus, help that girl. She loved Tameka like a sister, but after this event was done, they were going to have to address the issues of their friendship.

Constance's thoughts were in a whirlwind, but she had to make sure to focus on the matter at hand and that was checking the address for the meeting. She went back into her office and retrieved the business card from her work bag.

She checked the address written on the back and was surprised to see that the address matched Ahyende's studio.

Loren Prescott

Curator

Washington D.C. Museum of Modern Art

She found it odd that he hadn't mentioned the meeting to her. She called him on his cell phone so he could fill her in on what was going on, but his phone went straight to voicemail. She didn't leave a message, figuring she would ask him about the secrecy of the meeting when she saw him.

On the drive over, she called Ayende one more time but, once again, his phone went straight to voicemail. Once she arrived at the studio, Constance sat in the car for a few minutes, taking deep breaths to calm herself down. She tended to overreact and didn't want to blow up at Ahyende for keeping his participation in the show a secret from her. "Maybe he doesn't know the show will be held at my shop," she thought aloud.

Constance rode the freight elevator up to Ahyende's studio. Standing outside the door, she could hear muffled voices from inside. She pressed the buzzer to be let in, but there was no answer, only the muffled voices. She pressed the buzzer two more times and waited for the door to open. This time, the muffled voices grew louder. She pressed the buzzer long and hard, allowing it to sound for a few seconds.

The door finally opened, and she was greeted by Loren. "Constance, how nice to see you. Do come in."

Constance was still perplexed. Ahyende was standing in the middle of the room looking highly upset.

"Ahyende, what is going on here?" Constance asked.

"It seems," Loren responded, "that you and my husband are having an affair."

Constance was confused. "You're *what*?"

"My *husband*," Loren reiterated. "Ahyende deserted me back in D.C., so I had to hire a private investigator to track him down. It took him some time but eventually, he located him. And imagine my surprise when I learned that the two of you have been sneaking around. Ahyende, you should really get some curtains for this place." She snickered.

Constance's face grew heated as she withheld her rage. "Ahyende, is this true?"

"Oh, honey, it's the God's honest truth," Loren replied, handing her their marriage certificate.

Constance examined the stamp and seal on the certificate closely to ensure it wasn't a fake.

"When I first met you that morning in the parking lot, I hadn't a clue as to who you were, but fate is funny like that. I'd met Ahyende there to talk about a reconciliation."

A mass of tears welled in Constance's eyes and plummeted down her cheeks. "Ahyende, how could you do this to me?" she cried.

"Constance, it's not what you think," Ahyende quickly retorted.

"So you aren't married to her?"

"Yes," he stammered, "Loren and I are married, but there's more to it than that."

"No, there isn't," Constance yelled. "You are, by law, and in the eyes of God, a married man, and you never bothered to tell me!"

Ahyende quickly walked over to Constance. "Connie, I was going to tell you when the time was right. Loren isn't telling you the whole truth. Back home, I found out she was having an affair, and I filed for divorce. She refuses to sign the divorce papers." He leaned in closer and tried to embrace her.

"Don't touch me! Don't you dare touch me," she screeched. "Do you have any idea how much I have given up to be with you? Here you are promising me the world, and you can't give it to me because you're married."

Ahyende stepped back. "What you've given up? Hmm? And what exactly have you given up, Constance? Last I checked, you're still engaged. For all I know, you could be screwing me *and* your fiancé."

Constance was infuriated. She slowly wiped the tears from her face and looked Ahyende squarely in the eyes. "Well, I guess that's something you will never know," she hissed and began to make her way to the door.

Before leaving, she shook Loren's hand. "Thank you, Mrs. Prescott, for this enlightening meeting, but it seems I will not be able to do business with your 'client.' I will show myself to the door."

Constance's brain was spinning. She was confused, heartbroken, and unsure of what to do next. Before exiting, she turned around to face Loren. "I guess we now know who vandalized my car."

"Vandalized your car?" Loren seemed puzzled. "I'm not sure what you're talking about, but I'm positive *I* didn't do it."

Constance was exasperated. "Three months ago, *you* keyed the word whore into my car and slashed all my tires!"

Loren let out a laugh. "I'd be lying if I said I didn't get any pleasure from hearing that, but I can swear on a stack of bibles that I didn't do it. I guess that's karma for you."

Constance slammed the door on her way out. Instinctively, she dialed Yvette to get her take on the situation but quickly remembered that she and Yvette were no longer on speaking terms and hung up. Calling Tameka was strictly out of the question. She would only relish in her unfortunate news. There was only one person to whom she could turn to rectify this situation.

Constance used her spare key to let herself into her parents' home. No one was in the living room, but she could hear the television playing in the den. "Mama! Daddy!" Constance called out despite the lump in her throat.

"We're back here," her mother replied.

Constance made a beeline to the den, finding her parents seated in their matching recliners, watching an episode of *Perry Mason*. She immediately collapsed her head onto her mother's lap and sobbed uncontrollably. Between breaths, she told her mother what happened between her, Ahyende, and Loren.

Mildred listened intently, caressing Constance's back as her daughter sat weeping at her feet. When Constance was all cried out and had run out of words, her father was the first to speak.

Mr. McGuire's voice was low and steady. "Cupcake, I know this man hurt you, but as I sit listening to you, I can't help but take some responsibility for your actions. To hear how you were able to hold all these secrets bottled up inside and keep your true feelings for Marvin a charade, cloaking your affections for another man in secrecy ... Just goes to show I haven't been the best role model for you." He removed his wire-framed glasses and massaged the corners of his eyes. "I took your mother through a lot, but I thought as long as things looked good on the surface, no one would ever find out, not the church, not your mother, and definitely not you. I was so wrong. Listening to you just now is as if I were hearing myself, reliving a life cascaded with lies and false appearances, too afraid to face my truth so I would rather live a lie. Constance, what I have done is wrong. I lied to you, myself, my wife, my congregation but, more importantly, I lied to God. How can a person who lives a life of righteousness on display be so full of sin in dark places? Darlin', you have to be honest with God first because you can lie to everyone else, even yourself, but you can't lie to Him."

Constance sat upright, hanging on to her father's every word.

"You can't play victim in this circumstance, not when you've also played a role in hurting others ... in hurting God. We are human, yes, and no person is without err, but to blatantly sin, well, that breaks the heart of the Lord and it grieves the Holy Spirit. Baby, you must come clean with God, and you must come clean to those you've wronged, too."

Constance knew her father was right, and as much as she hated the thought of telling Marvin, she knew she had to. Too much time had already passed, too many lies had been told. How could she possibly be angry with Ahyende for playing a game she was playing also? "Daddy, can you pray with me?"

"Of course, baby."

Constance, Gerald, and Mildred all held hands and prayed together as a family. Constance said a special prayer for the courage to face Marvin and tell him the truth. After the prayer, Gerald placed a loving kiss upon his daughter's head before she headed out the door.

With so much commotion, Constance had forgotten she was meeting Marvin for dinner. *I will tell him then,* she thought. *It's a public place, so he won't cause a scene.*

She arrived at her condo, quickly showered, and slipped into a form-fitting black spaghetti-strap dress and a pair of black stilettos. Her hair was bone straight, and she wore a simple part down the middle. Before leaving, she put her engagement ring on, as not to alarm Marvin, and headed out the door.

Constance pulled into the parking lot of the packed

restaurant. The valets were moving quickly like little worker ants who were all wearing the same outfit. She pulled up front to valet her car, gave them the keys, and walked inside. She approached the hostess and gave her Marvin's name. Constance inhaled and exhaled deeply as she followed the hostess to Marvin's table. They had a booth by the window overlooking the city.

Marvin was on the phone when she arrived. He seemed to be in a heated discussion but quickly hung up once he noticed her. He placed his phone in his pocket and stood up to greet Constance. "Good evening, my love."

"Hello, Marvin. Trouble at work?"

"Nothing I can't handle," he replied coolly as he got up to pull back her chair. He placed a single kiss on Constance's cheek and sat. "Well, you sure are a sight for sore eyes."

"Thank you." Constance blushed. "You don't look bad yourself. New suit?"

He leaned back and revealed a smug smile. "Why, yes. When you make partner, you must look your absolute best. This suit cost me close to three thousand dollars, but it was worth every penny. I'm telling you, Connie, this move to partner is going to put our lives in a new trajectory. We're well on our way to Washington."

Just then, Marvin's cell rang. He looked at the screen and took the phone call immediately. "I'm sorry, but I'm going to have to call you back ... I know it's important, but I'm having dinner with my gorgeous fiancée ... I'll call you back Monday. We can talk business then."

Constance couldn't believe her ears. In all his years at the firm, Marvin had never turned down a business call. He raised his wine glass and offered it up for a toast.

"To us. From college sweethearts to the next Barack and Michelle Obama."

Constance raised her glass. "To us."

She was beginning to think that perhaps things were turning around for them. After all, it seemed things weren't going to manifest between her and Ahyende. Maybe this was God's way of showing her that she and Marvin belonged together.

Constance decided to hold off on her confession. She'd made up her mind to see things through with Marvin. He may not have been the heartthrob she longed for, but he was safe and a good provider. As long as she had that, everything else would fall into place.

CHAPTER TWELVE

... Comes to Light

After dinner, Constance and Marvin went back to her place. They made love, and Marvin quickly drifted to sleep. Familiar feelings began to revisit: uneasiness, restlessness, dissatisfaction.

Get it together, Connie. Sex isn't the most important thing in a relationship.

Constance spooned Marvin and finally fell asleep. As she slept, she dreamed she was in her father's church dressed in an all-white wedding dress, a veil covering her face obstructing her view. Through the veil, she could make out the faces of her family and friends who were all smiling, except her mother, who was crying uncontrollably. There was also a baby wailing. The sounds of her mother and the baby's cries were drowning out her father's words as he presided.

"What, Daddy? I can't hear you," Constance shouted.

Her father continued talking in a muffled tone, and the cries only grew louder. Constance yelled over the voices. "Daddy! Daddy! I can't hear you!"

Her father just continued, and the cries began to echo. Slowly, Constance's veil began to rise. The cries increased. The higher the veil rose, the louder the cries grew, and the lights in the church started to dim.

Darkness engulfed the room.

"Stop! Stop!" she screamed, but no one stopped.

At the final rise of the veil, Constance jolted out of her sleep, her chest heaving, her body covered in perspiration. "What the hell!" she said to herself.

She went downstairs to grab a drink of water and make sense of her dream. *Come on, Constance, get it together. It's just nerves. You and Marvin ... You're gonna be okay ... We're gonna be okay.*

As she finished her water and began making her way back upstairs, there was a knock at the door. Constance checked the time. It was a little past midnight, and she didn't know who could possibly be at her door this late. Her heart skipped a beat.

Ahyende?

Constance paused for a moment, not wanting to seem too anxious, but the knock came again, this time, at a frantic pace. She looked upstairs to see if Marvin had awakened and was making his way down, but there was no sign he had been roused. Quickly, she made her way to the door and peered through the peephole. It was Tameka. Puzzled, Constance opened the door.

"Hey, girl. What you doing here so late? Everything okay?"

"Oh, yeah, it's fine. I just got off a date with this guy, and I faked an emergency and told him to drop me off here. Your place was closer to the restaurant, and I didn't want to spend another moment with him."

"Was it that bad?" Constance laughed as she let Tameka in.

"Worse."

"Girl, the way you were knocking, I thought you were gonna wake Marvin."

Tameka nonchalantly surveyed the room. "Oh, Marvin's here?"

"Yeah. We went out to dinner and had a really nice time. During dinner, he even declined a business call for me. Told them he was with his fiancée and he'd get back to them Monday. Can you believe that?"

"No, I can't. Sounds like Marvin may be turning over a new leaf. So does that mean you're done with that island man?"

"Girl, he and I are so done. I can't go into details now, but he wasn't who I thought he was. It's for the best, though, because Marvin and I have history, and that isn't something you throw away for someone you just met."

"I guess not," Tameka replied, slowly pacing the room.

"Let me grab you some blankets. You can camp out in the office if you like." Constance made her way to the hall closet. "So what's up with this guy you were out with?" she called out over her shoulder.

Tameka sat on the sofa and ran her hands through her hair. "Not much," she replied with a sigh. "He was just broke and boring."

Constance made her way back into the living room, blankets in hand. "Girl, you and wanting these men with money. That usher, Jermaine, didn't have any money, and you were all over him, although that didn't last long. The last time I talked to you, you told me you'd met someone else. What happened with that?" Constance set the blankets down on the sofa.

Tameka placed her handbag on the sofa next to her and took off her stilettos, placing them neatly in front of her. "Oh, that? It seems he'd rather be with his whore of a girlfriend instead. She cheated on him, and instead of leaving her trifling ass, he decided to marry the bitch," she hissed.

"Whoa, that's harsh. You must have really liked this guy."

"I did," Tameka replied, rising from the sofa. "I still do. I-I-I fell in love with him." Tears began to roll down Tameka's cheeks.

Constance walked over to her friend and gave her a hug. "Oh, MeMe, it's okay. You'll find the right guy. It just takes time," she said, meaning every word.

Tameka raised her head, her eyes red and swollen. "What hurts the most is that even after I showed him that this woman is a two-timing whore, he still wouldn't leave her."

Constance was concerned. "MeMe, what did you do? What do you mean you *showed* him?"

Tameka's lips curled as she looked Constance squarely in the eyes. "I found out she was cheating on him, so I hired someone to vandalize her car. They slashed her tires and spray painted WHORE all over it, and when she told him what happened, he still didn't leave. He didn't have one inkling that his precious green-eyed beauty was cheating on him with some third-world island nigga."

Constance was in shock, her head spinning from Tameka's confession. Slowly, she backed up. "It was *you*? All this time?"

Tameka chuckled. "Yes, you high-yellow princess. It was me."

"But why would you do that to me? We've been best friends since we were kids."

"And the whole world has been kissing your ass since we were kids!" Tameka's voice elevated, her tone stern. "You always had everything, and I had nothing. I've lived my entire life in your shadow. Well, finally, I had a chance to have something that was yours, and he still chose you in the end! And then tonight, after we had spent an *amazing* weekend together in Miami, he dismissed my call and told me he'll talk to me Monday, so he could have dinner with his slutty fiancé!"

Constance's face grew red, and she took a hard swallow before yelling, "Tameka, get the hell out of my house!"

Tameka moved closer to Constance, their noses practically touching. "I'm not leaving until I get what I came for," she said right before serving Constance a ferocious right hook to the jaw.

The punch knocked Constance off balance, and she tumbled over the coffee table, landing on her back, hitting her head on the wooden floor.

"I came here for my man, and I'm not leaving without him!" Tameka ran over to Constance and knelt over her, preparing to deliver another blow, but Constance moved swiftly, striking her in the face, splitting Tameka's lip.

Blood flowed freely. They tussled on the floor. Tameka pulled Constance's hair, provoking Constance to slap Tameka with a blow so forceful it left a handprint across her ebony skin.

The commotion awakened Marvin, who ran downstairs. He stood at the bottom of the stairs frozen, unsure of what was going on. "Tameka, what the hell are you doing?"

The sound of Marvin's voice surprised Tameka and she released Constance. She stood, exposing a mouth full of blood. "Hey, baby! I came here looking for you." She used the back of her hand to wipe the blood from her mouth. Her demeanor was much calmer now. "You weren't acting like yourself tonight, so I came to see what the problem was. And now I know it was this bitch occupying your time." She gestured toward Constance. "But you don't have to worry about that anymore because she knows all about us, and now we can be together."

Marvin crept across the room and made his way toward her. "Tameka, this is crazy. You don't have to do this.

I know you and I had a thing, but I love Constance," he said moving cautiously. "She and I are going to get married. I hate to have to tell you this way, but you need to know that Constance is the woman I choose."

Constance eased her way off the floor and limped toward Marvin, wincing from the throbbing pain in her back.

Tameka looked bewildered and began crying hysterically. "You don't know what you're saying! You don't know what she's done!" She looked over at Constance, who was inching closer to Marvin. "Don't you take another step!" Tameka snapped.

"MeMe, please, this is crazy. Look, just go home. I won't call the police, and we can talk about this in a day or two when we've had time to calm down and collect our thoughts."

Marvin moved closer to Constance. "Tameka, please just go home. I'll call you later, and we'll talk about this."

"So, you aren't coming with me?" She began to sob.

"No, I'm not. Constance is hurt and bleeding. I'm going to take her to the emergency room." Marvin put his arm around Constance's waist.

Tameka began to pace the floor frantically, and she released a bloodcurdling scream. "Why is everything always about Constance? I'm bleeding, too! I'm hurt! Why don't you love me, Marvin? I'd never hurt you the way she did. I'd never cheat on you."

Marvin froze. "What?"

Tameka let out a menacing cackle. "She's cheating on

you, Marvin, and has been for the past three months. She's been seeing some man she met at her father's church since you proposed to her. See, she doesn't love you. She's just a whore, a lying, cheating whore!"

Marvin looked at Constance, who was in tears. "Is this true, Connie?"

"Yes ... yes, it's true. I wanted to tell you, but I didn't know how. But it's all over now. Things ended between us. You're the man I want to be with." Constance wasn't sure she believed those words but, right now, all she wanted was to get Tameka out of her house, and she'd say whatever was necessary to accomplish that.

Marvin paused. He was beginning to feel light headed. "I need to sit down." He made his way to the armchair and sat, placing his head in his hands. He took a deep breath before speaking. "It's okay. We'll work this out. We'll get counseling. It'll be okay. We both made terrible mistakes, but we'll get through this."

Tameka was not pleased with Marvin's response. She reached underneath her dress and pulled out a small pistol. "No!" she shrieked. "She doesn't get to win! I came here for you, and if I can't have you, neither can she."

Tameka raised the pistol and pointed it at Constance. Constance's eyes grew wide, and her body froze with fear.

Marvin began to panic. "Tameka, what are you doing? You aren't thinking clearly. Put the gun down." He inched closer to Constance, who still couldn't move. "You don't want to do this."

"Don't tell me what I don't want to do! Tameka was

locked in on Constance. "For as long as I can remember, she has been a constant reminder of everything I don't have. The looks, the career, the family." Tameka sobbed. "Why couldn't it have been me?"

Constance finally spoke. "MeMe, you have your career, your parents, and your friends. We all love you. Please don't do this. You have too much to lose. Please ... put ... the gun ... down."

Tameka shifted from her haze. "It's too late."

Pop!

Pop!

Pop!

The synchronistic beeping awakened Constance. She tried to move, but the stabbing pain in her chest was debilitating. Her throat was sore, and her mouth was dry. She tried to speak but was met with a hushed whisper.

"Shh, shh. Don't speak. I'm so glad you're finally up, baby."

Constance recognized the voice as her mother's. She looked around the room and saw that her mother and Yvette were there. Constance smiled at her friend. "Yvette," she whispered.

"It's okay, Connie. It's okay," Yvette said between sobs.

"Where's—"

"Marie is fine. She's with her father." Yvette's smile faded. "We're getting a

divorce. You were right."

Constance casted her eyes downward.

"It's okay. Honestly, I kind of knew all along. He was always on that laptop late at night, so I put in some spyware. Turns out, he was looking at gay porn. I was just hormonal and in denial, and I took it out on you. But enough about that. I'm glad you're okay. I don't know what I would do if ... if ..." Yvette began to cry. She sat next to Constance on the hospital bed and gave her a hug. "You're like a sister to me, and I couldn't imagine my life without you in it."

Mr. McGuire entered the room with a doctor. Marvin followed slowly, his arm in a sling.

Immediately, tears filled Constance's eyes. Her throat didn't seem so sore and dry anymore, and she was finally able to speak a little clearer. "Marvin," was all she could manage in a voice slightly above a whisper.

The two embraced and cried.

"It's okay. I'm fine. You're fine. Everything is going to be okay," he assured her.

Constance looked him over and noticed the sling. "What exactly happened?"

"Hi, I'm Dr. Thomas." The young doctor extended his hand to greet Constance. "You received a gunshot wound to the chest. You lost a lot of blood but, overall, you are quite lucky. Once the bullet hit, it lost velocity and didn't hit any major organs. Your fiancé took a hit to the shoulder, lunging toward you to block the shot."

Her eyes began to well. "Marvin, you put your life on the line ... for *me*?"

Marvin gave her a soft kiss on the lips. "And I'd do it again if I had to."

Constance stared off for a moment, trying to take in all the information. Her head was spinning with questions that needed to be answered. She examined Marvin's wound. "But I heard *three* shots."

The room grew silent. Mrs. McGuire held Constance's hand. "Baby, Tameka took her own life."

"No!" Constance wailed. "This is all my fault! It's all my fault! If I hadn't been so deceptive, so wrapped up in my own life, I could've helped her. Why? Why didn't I take the time to see that she was hurting?"

Marvin enveloped her in his arms. "It's okay," he whispered. "We both made mistakes." He placed a kiss on Constance's forehead. "No one could have ever seen this coming."

A dead silence fell over the room. No one dared say a word. They all just allowed Constance the time to mourn her best friend.

A knock at the door interrupted the stillness.

Constance looked up from Marvin's embrace. "Ahyende!" Her voice was filled with both excitement and curiosity while an uneasiness settled into the room.

"I'm sorry," said Yvette. "I saw him at church Sunday and told him what happened."

Mrs. McGuire threw her a disapproving look.

"It's okay," Constance replied.

"Hello, everyone," Ahyende said. "Pastor, First Lady."

Embarrassment blanketed Constance's face.

Marvin eased the tension. "Hi, I'm Marvin, Constance's fiancé." He extended his good hand and offered a handshake.

"I apologize. I didn't want to intrude. I just wanted to check on Constance. Make sure she's okay."

"I'm fine, I guess."

"Constance is healing nicely, especially for a person who was shot at such close range," Dr. Thomas said. "And there was no harm to the baby."

"*Baby!*" everyone shouted in synchrony.

Dr. Thomas bore a look of regret. "My sincerest apologies. I just assumed ..." The doctor's face turned crimson.

"How far along am I?" Constance asked.

"According to the ultrasound, you're approximately eight weeks, which is usually around the time you get to hear the baby's heartbeat. We can arrange that if you like."

Constance was beyond belief. "I'd like that very much."

"Well, let me put in an order, and hopefully we can have that done today." The doctor left the room.

Constance burst into tears of joy. She touched her stomach and looked at her parents. "I'm going to have a baby."

Yvette ran over to her. "This is so exciting! Our kids are going to grow up together!"

The two began to imagine the lives their babies would share. They talked about playdates and how they would be best friends and go to the same school.

Mrs. McGuire cleared her throat. "Aren't we forgetting something?" She glared at Ahyende with a side eye.

Constance and Yvette's excitement quickly faded. The tension between Ahyende and Marvin was thick and unsettling.

Mr. McGuire groaned. "Why did you have to go and ruin the mood, Mildred?"

Mrs. McGuire looked appalled. "I only pointed out what these two men were obviously thinking, what we are *all* thinking."

"Well, I wasn't." Mr. McGuire's tone was stern and gruff. "All I know is that my one and only child is having a baby, I'm going to be a grandfather, and you'll be a grandmother. Why can't we just focus on that? These past two days have been nothing but pure hell, filled with devastation and grief. Let us just take a moment to relish in some happy news."

"Thank you, Daddy." Constance blew her father a kiss.

"I love you, cupcake. Now, let's get out of here so Connie and my grandbaby can get some rest." Mr. McGuire leaned over and gave Constance a forehead kiss. "Let's go, Mildred."

Mrs. McGuire kissed her daughter and followed her husband. Yvette gave Constance one more hug and promised to come back tomorrow and visit.

Marvin and Ahyende were the only ones left. For a moment, all that stood between them was an uncomfortable silence.

Marvin spoke first. "So whose is it?"

Ahyende was offended. "Hey, man, do you really think this is the time? She could've died for Christ's sake."

"You don't have to tell me! I was there. I put my life on the line for hers, and I'd do it again. That's how much I love her. But what I won't stand for is being a laughing stock." Marvin looked intently at Constance. "I won't stand for you embarrassing me. I'm not going to raise another man's baby, and I'm not going to sit around for seven months hoping this kid is mine."

Constance was irate. "So what exactly are you saying?"

"What I'm saying is the only people who know about this baby are in this room. Not even my own mother knows—thank God. You can just get it taken care of, and after the wedding, we can try again."

Constance couldn't believe what she was hearing. "What!"

Ahyende was incredulous. "Man, are you suggesting that your future wife and mother of your child have an abortion?"

"That's precisely what I'm saying."

Ahyende stood toe to toe with Marvin. He towered him by size and stature, standing about a foot taller. He clenched his hand into a fist. "The only reason I'm not going to hit you right now is because I love the woman lying in that hospital bed. And whether the baby is mine or yours, I'm going to stick around because this child is going to need a proper example of what a man is."

Marvin cackled. "Look, Connie, you've got a choice to make. We're both young. We can try again, but this—this isn't part of our plan. I can get past what you've done, but I'm not living with a daily reminder." Marvin's remark took Constance back to her childhood. Here stood Marvin echoing the words of her mother to her father all those years ago. She had become exactly what she tried so hard not to be.

"Man, you are a *real* piece of work," Ahyende growled.

Marvin was unfazed with a smug look on his face. "Unlike you, I'm a man who knows what he wants, a man who knows how to get things done. It's the reason Constance fell for me, and it's the reason she chose to stay with me."

Constance finally spoke up. "That's not why I chose you."

Marvin was taken aback. "What?"

She propped herself up in her bed. "I said, that's not why I chose you. Marvin, you are a pompous, self-centered, egotistical mama's boy. You constantly neglect my needs and wants, and you have no clue as to what it is I want to do with my life. You didn't even know that I was opening a new location for the boutique. You never cared about me or what I wanted. Not once did you even ask. You have always treated me like a prize, a light-skinned token that you parade around and wear like a status symbol. The only reason I broke things off with Ahyende is because I found out he was still legally married. So I figured being with you was safer and less scary than starting over with someone else."

Marvin shook his head and chuckled. "All that beauty

and no brains. You think your little confession bothers me? Do you really want to know why I was so forgiving of what you've done? Do you think Tameka was the only one? Hell, she was just something to pass the time. I could sense how jealous she was of you, and I knew she'd do anything to stick it to you—and I mean *anything*. I guess I should've known that the bitch was crazy, but I never thought she would try to kill you. All because I didn't want her. I couldn't take her dark ass to Capitol Hill. But you ... you've got that non-threatening look. White folks fall over backwards for a yella girl. Constance, I could get ten of you. Hell, I've had at least fifteen. As a matter of fact, I have a Swedish girl waiting on me back at my place who is more than happy to ride the sidelines until she can give me a pretty mulatto baby. You, my dear, were just a pit stop on my way to the top."

Constance listened to Marvin, unnerved. A few months ago, his words would have cut her like razor blades. But today was a new day. She had experienced far too much to be consumed with Marvin's antics. She looked at him and simply said, "Good luck with that."

Marvin sauntered out of the hospital room just as smug as ever.

Ahyende sat near Constance on the bed. He placed his hand on her stomach. "I'm going to be the best dad, and we're going to be amazing parents."

Constance placed her hand on top of Ahyende's. "Just because I'm not with Marvin doesn't mean I chose you."

Ahyende was confused.

"Ahyende, you lied to me. Whether she was cheating or if you signed the divorce papers, it doesn't matter. When it's all said and done, you put me in a position that I never wanted to be in, and you took away my right to choose. I'm sure you will be a great father, and we would be amazing parents, but the only person I'm choosing is my baby. That is my priority."

Ahyende hung his head with visible heartache. "I understand," he said. "I don't like it, but I respect it. Just know that I'm never going anywhere. I'm here for you, and I'm here for that baby. A love like ours is rare, and I'm not giving that up easily. I'm going to fight for you, for both of you, and I apologize for the wrong I've done to you."

Ahyende gave Constance one final kiss and left the hospital room. For the first time in her life, Constance had made a decision on her own accord. She was going to live her life the best way she thought fit. Knowing it wouldn't be easy, she was prepared to raise her child on her own; and she didn't give a damn about what anyone else thought.

Constance placed her hand on her stomach, smiled, and hummed a lullaby until she fell asleep.

Thank you for reading *If It Isn't Love.* If you've enjoyed this book, please help spread the word and leave an online review.
Thank you!

CONNECT WITH TANYA TAYLOR

Learn more about Tanya Taylor and her work
www.authortanyataylor.com

Connect with Tanya Taylor on social media
Instagram: @authortanyataylor
Facebook: facebook.com/authortanyataylor.5

Made in the USA
Columbia, SC
12 December 2019